Contemptible <u>Blue</u>

Written by Lucas Gardner

Cover design by Mikey Heller

Copyright © Lucas Gardner

Sex Productions 2017

Queens, NY

Contents

Ishmael..*1*

Know Thy Enemy...*4*

A Sermon..*16*

I Don't Like You And You Don't

    Like Me...*20*

A Fine Day To Go A-Whalin'.............................*30*

Please Don't Tell Anyone

    About This...*37*

Downtime & Good Omens....................................*49*

Harpoon-Man...*53*

First Aid..*62*

Your Worst Night-Maritime................................*65*

My Behemoth, My Bane,

    My Contemptible Blue..................................*68*

Slaughter on The Ted...*75*

Milton Died..*85*

The Hold...*96*

Psychological Warfare.......................................*101*

Lower Yer Harpoon...*105*

This Ship Was Never Yours................................*111*

Dead Man's Float...*118*

The Confederacy For The

    War On Whalers.............................125

Don't Trust The Captain....................128

Whaleship USS Maine.......................133

G O D 'S W O R K.............................139

Get A Load Of THIS

    Motherfucker, Right!?..................148

The Confederacy Falls......................154

You Seriously Fucked Dale?

    Are You Fucking Shitting Me?......163

Was He As Beautiful As They

    Say?..169

There Is A Gigantic Hole Inside

    Of Me...176

Beowulf..184

The 15th Annual Kurd Clams

    N' Shanties Seaside Festival........190

HP-20003F...196

30 Days 'Til Whaling Season............208

A Mere Canaller In A

    Nantucketer's Clothing................214

The Blue Crew...................................223

Thar She Blows!.................................235

Captain Fortnight Talks

    To Jojo..244

What's Up, My 'Pooners?...................................246

Stubborn Captains Sink Ships............................256

Chilled To The Bone...260

The Stateroom..276

The Golden Boy..287

Happy Birthday Dudley.....................................296

I'll Suck the Marrow

    Out Thy Bones...302

An Order Is An Order.......................................310

Sex With A Woman..314

Hootenanny...319

Onion Island...332

Contemptible Blue

I.

Ishmael

"Don't call me Ishmael," I told my therapist, who'd just called me Ishmael for some reason.

"Sorry," she said, "I've been re-reading *Moby Dick*. The main character's name is Ishmael. I guess I have 'Ishmael' on the brain. Have you read it? I think you'd appreciate it. It's about the obsessive nature of man, about longing to be the victor no matter the cost—things you might understand."

I promptly fired my therapist and stormed out of her office, because if I wanted to pay $150 an hour for someone to talk to me about books, I'd join an expensive book club. Then, when it was time to pay, I'd keep saying, "Sorry, forgot my wallet. I'll get you next book club meeting, for sure."

Contemptible Blue

I went to the local library and ripped a couple pages out of an old copy of *Moby Dick* and brought them home to read. I figured I'd take a look to see if I could figure out what the doctor was getting at. I had never heard of this "Moby Dick," but the name was funny enough so I decided to give it a shot. I had trouble making sense of the writing (I must have stolen a bad translation), but from what I could glean, the book was about a virgin named Ishmael who sails out to sea on a big boat to help kill a whale. To my surprise, the tale did indeed "speak" to me. Something about the idea of destroying a big, powerful, noble creature of the ocean for no reason really made sense. If you could pull that off, then you could pull off *anything*. The teamwork aspect of whaling was unappealing, but the rest was good.

I was coming off a streak of bad luck in the American West that I'd rather not revisit right now, and I really needed a vacation. I work really hard. I knew what I had to do to get myself out of this rut I'd been in—what I had to do to feel "whole." I had to go kill a big whale, for no reason.

Why is it that *every* man, after ripping a few pages out of a library copy of *Moby Dick* and reading them out of order, dreams of the sea? Why is that such a universal experience? I couldn't say. All I knew was that, deep down, my heart was telling me I needed to go do this.

This is gonna rule, I thought to myself as I began the 50-mile walk to the nearest whaling town. *Mad whales 'bout to die!*

I made a quick stop at the local nautical supply store to pick myself up a harpoon before my big nautical adventure, but just like at all the other nautical supply stores in the area, there was a big sign hung on the storefront with my picture on it that said: "Do NOT sell this man a harpoon." I crossed the word "not" out on the sign and tried to go in and buy a harpoon, but the clerk wasn't fooled. "*You* just lost a sale," I told the guy, flashing a one dollar bill at him, even though that wasn't enough money to buy a harpoon.

I went to a pawn shop across the street and traded my wedding ring for a harpoon, then I was all set. *Watch out, whales,* I thought to myself.

II.

Know Thy Enemy

On my way to Skalego I decided to stop at the library again to rent out some books about whales. Know thy enemy, and all that. I asked the librarian where the whales section was and she said, "The cetology section is in the basement." She was a bad librarian—I specifically asked for the *whales* section.

I looked around for hours before I finally found the whales books. They were in the basement, in a section that was marked "Cetology" for some reason. The books were a little wordy for my tastes. I prefer literature that's primarily picture-based. See, that's the one thing the ancient Egyptians got right. I started to storm out of the library because I was pissed off for some reason, then on the way out I spotted a nautical dictionary and snatched it so that I would be able to communicate with the other sailors on my upcoming whaling adventure. I didn't know much of the nautical lingo—only the basics, like, "Ahoy!" and, "Thar she blows!" and, "¡Ay dios mio, big poppa loves to fish!" and I wasn't even completely sure what those expressions meant.

I had never met a sailor or even been on a boat or seen a fish in person before, so I was going to be pretty "green" going into this whole experience, but I always suspected that I was made for the sea, as of that morning. Pretty much all you have to do to be a sailor is find a boat and stand on it, which seemed easy. Although I guess you *are* drunk the whole time, so maybe it was a little hard. *I'll be fine,* I thought to myself.

After leaving a real quick essay of poor feedback that was longer than this novel in the library suggestion box, I left and finished the walk to Skalego. "Thar she blows!" I yelled no reason.

I had heard tales of the famous Skalego. It was a tiny little town on the coast that was supposedly a hub for some of the best sailors in the world. I'd be sure to find a good crew of whalers there. Even if not, they had a good porno theater I'd been meaning to check out.

After a lengthy trek I finally arrived at Skalego, where the streets were lined with shops, inns, schools and churches. It was a quiet, dull, safe little town—it'd be an awful place to raise a family. I wandered the dampened cobblestone streets for a while until I spotted a small tavern that looked like it might be a local whaler's hangout. It was called The Seaman's Drip. Once I finished laughing at the funny tavern name (it was *seriously* called that!!!) I was ready to go in and fraternize with some of my fellow men of the sea, or at the very least get drunk.

I entered the tavern and was overcome with a certain feeling of culture shock. The place was full of big, burly, bearded old men guzzling booze at the bar, all looking like they'd been to war a thousand times over. They had a certain grizzled quality to them that was slightly intimidating. I worried they might see right through me if I tried to "hang" with them. If so, they'd never let me join their crew. Or even worse: they'd hire me as the guy whose job it was to swab the deck, or whatever. *If anyone tries to make me swab the deck I'm gonna be pissed off,* I thought to myself. I was pretty sure that being the guy who swabs the deck was, like, the *worst* guy you could be on the boat.

I just had to do my best to make an

impressive entrance and assert myself as an able shipmate. "Ahoy!" I exclaimed, commanding a hush over the crowd. "Which of ye be whalers? It's been a fortnight since I've gone a-whalin' and I long for the sea! Thar she blows, indeed! Oh, how I long to taste that salty ocean air once again! I implore ye, ye lily-livered scoundrels: please, please hang out with me."

I felt great about my entrance, and expected the guys to throw me the keys to their boats and practically *beg* me to whale for them, but they didn't seem fooled. They all took a quiet moment to size me up, staring me down from head to foot, and they didn't seem impressed. They were all giving me these cold, quizzical looks that seemed to say, *This looks like the type of guy that I'd make swab the deck.* "I ain't swabbin' *shit*," I announced preemptively.

"Welcome to The Seaman's Drip, coward!" one of them finally said.

Contemptible Blue

"Blessed evening, coward," another one said.

"Coward ho!" another said.

I froze up. I had never been rejected so swiftly or so harshly before. Even wielding my expensive harpoon, and even after employing what I thought was very careful use of the word "fortnight," I was immediately reduced to a "coward" by the very men I was desperately relying on to get me out to sea. "Welp, never mind," I said, already giving up on this whole whaling thing. "This was a mistake. See you guys later. I'm gonna go hit up that porno theater."

I turned around to leave and go return my harpoon, then I felt a hand on my shoulder. I turned around and lumbering over me was a slouched, white-haired old man whose face appeared to have been chewed off by something. "Where ye rushin' off to with such haste, coward?" he asked. "Seat yourself—please!—and enjoy a drink. A small beer, on me. Aye! Let The Seaman's Drip quench your thirst."

"Ha ha ha," I said. Then I said, "I'm just looking for a crew of sailors to join. I'm a whalin' man."

The faceless old sailor erupted into laughter, his breath stinking of liquor and fish, like mine. "There is no company I relish more than the humble company of a coward with a sense of humor," he said. "It's been a wretched month, this one, and I've wept more than a good man ought to in an entire lifetime. Aye! What I needed this evenin', my friend, was indeed a hearty laugh. I thank ye. Now then, what's yer real rank? A mere, lowly swabbie? Me too! Ye'll find good company here at The Drip!"

"What?"

"Are ye new in Skalego, lad? This is the tavern of the local coward, where the town's cowards, and only *they*, come to drink. I myself jumped overboard during my last voyage at sea 'cause the boat made a scary noise. Got my face, homely as it was, chewed off by a school of crabs! If ye're a proper sailor—one of high esteem—then ye've come to the wrong tavern."

"Coward's tavern?" I asked. "You mean this is where the bad sailors hang out?"

"Aye!" he said.

"What did you say your nautical ranking was again?" I asked.

"We're swabbies."

"What do swabbies do?"

"Swab the deck."

"*Nope. No way,*" I said, turning around and storming out of the tavern.

I couldn't get away from those pathetic, low-ranking deck swabbers fast enough. Just from being around them I felt so dirty that I wanted to *shower*, at some point within the next few weeks.

I wandered around Skalego a little more,

eventually following the sound of waves to the ocean shore. I spotted a doddering old fisherman trying to get his fishing hook untangled from a big clump of seaweed. "Damn this cursed, wretched seaweed," he muttered to himself. I went up to him and asked him where I might find a good whaling crew around Skalego. "Thy luck hath run out, lad," the bad fisherman told me, "for whaling season began one month ago. Any learned whaler, with high hopes in his heart for a prosperous whaling voyage, hath been asea for that amount of time."

"A month? Ah yes, about two fortnights," I said.

"Aye," he said, not giving me any credit for using "fortnight" back there.

"That's a shame," I continued. "I'm lookin' to go a-whalin'."

"Ahh," the fisherman moaned, "so thou fancy thyself a man of the sea?"

"Yes, I'm a whaler now. I mean, I'm a

whaler."

"Well, lad, if thou treasure thy longevity and thy good health more than a payday—august though thy pay may be—then thou wouldst not dare depart these peaceful shores, anyhow," the fisherman told me. "A tempestuous storm is soon due to sweepeth in from the West. Aye, a squall so raging it shall ravage even ships blessed by God himself."

"Uhh, actually, I'm an *atheist*," I asserted, bravely.

"Okay," he said.

"Now look here, lad," I continued, hoping the fisherman didn't notice me peaking at my nautical dictionary when I said "lad," "I'm a man of the sea, and no storm in the world is gonna keep me off the water."

The fisherman chuckled. "I suppose that when a whaler hears the siren call of the alluring sea, there is no hope in teth'rin' him to dry land," he said. "I suppose I need not remindeth thee: the sea can be a cruel mistress. Ah, the sea! 'Tis a turf eternally disputed by the Lord and the Devil alike, for it can be heavenly or it can be Hell."

I tried to explain to the fisherman that I don't necessarily believe in the afterlife as it's described biblically and that I don't care for how religion fails to acknowledge moral gray areas, but he didn't seem to be in the mood for a theological debate. He must have known he was outwitted. "Listen," I continued, "I've got my heart set on this trip."

"Aye!" the fisherman said with a slight smirk. "From a man who fancies himself a man of the sea—that most stubborn sort—what more couldst I hath expected? I suppose thee too, like thy fellow stubborn sailors, looketh down on us more grounded men—land lubbing men like myself who only wish to live long enough to watch our sons and our daughters grow. Thou heareth dire warnings of dangers asea beyond the offing, but the siren call of the sea rings louder in thy ear, doth it not? Thou dreameth of the sea and of only that," he said, reciting his thesis for his Take A Long Time To Say A Thing 101 class.

"Okay, well, I guess I'll—" I began to say.

"Ah, the sea!" the fisherman interrupted, pretty much just talking to himself at this point. "What troubled territory, for she—"

"Well, anyway, whatever," I said as I turned around to leave. "See ya later."

"Wait, hear me now, brave sailor," he said. "If thou so desperately wish to ship out to sea, despite having already missed a month of good whaling, thou shalt find thyself scraps of a crew at The Seaman's Drip, though it'd be mad to enlist the help of such inadequate men. I myself would never wish to handle such seamen, for that would be too much to swallow."

"Ha ha ha, holy shit," I said, laughing at the

fisherman's funny sentence. It's cool how sometimes humor can transcend the language barrier.

Then I got upset, realizing my only option was to join that crew of cowardly old deck swabbers. I said goodbye to the autistic fisherman and began making my way back to The Seaman's Drip, laughing the whole way there—I was excited to read the funny sign again.

III.

A Sermon

On my way back to the swabbie tavern, I came upon a large church with a sign hung above the front door that read: "ALL ARE WELCOME." I guess not all signs can be funny. From outside, I could hear the preacher howling in there. "The Lord shall watch over thee in times of peril," he declared, "but only if thou do thy due diligence unto him." Then he said something about how "to live a life of kindness and courage is to reject all influence of the Devil," so I went in there to tell the preacher that I don't necessarily believe in the afterlife as it's described biblically and that I don't care for how religion fails to acknowledge moral gray areas. *He's gonna hate this!* I thought to myself, excited for some reason.

It was a full house—men, women and children of all ages lined the pews and all were deeply moved by the words of the impassioned preacher. I took a seat in the back pew. "This oughta be good!" I called out sarcastically, elbowing the guy next to me. He asked me to be quiet.

"Thou cannot banish the Devil from thy life simply by pretending he is not there! Thou must invite the Lord into thy heart!" spoke the preacher.

"Amen!" someone shouted.

"Um, well, *actually*, I'm an *atheist,* so..." I

yelled aloud, being brave.

"And now, my dear friends," the preacher continued, "we shall acknowledge a recent tragedy —a tragedy that weighs oppressively on all our fragile hearts. Let us mourn the death of our dear friend, Captain Blagg. Let us mourn, yes, but let us not forget that the great Captain Blagg rests peacefully now in the Lord's eternal kindgom."

"Uhh, well, *actually*," I yelled out, "I don't necessarily believe in the afterlife as it's described biblically and I don't care for how religion fails to acknowledge moral gray areas. So..."

"Hush!" someone up front yelled.

"Thou in the back," the preacher yelled out, "thou art a stranger to me. Welcome. Art thou a loved one of Captain Blagg's?"

"*Who?*" I asked.

The preacher sighed. "Thou art new in town, it would seem," he said. "Welcome to the service. Today, we biddeth farewell to our friend

Captain Blagg, who struck joy into the hearts of all whom he met. We used to say the Devil himself could sink no ship so long as the great Captain Blagg was at its helm. But alas, it would seem the great captain has perished asea."

"Uh, okay, well," I said, "I think the Devil is more of a *social construct*, and—"

"Enough!" the preacher commanded.

"Okay, well, I'm feeling a little excluded, and—"

"That is *quite* enough!" the preacher cried again. "Let us sayeth now our final goodbyes to a great man, for we handeth him over now to the Lord!"

"Well actually, I feel like 'God' is just a *concept* created by *man* in order to—"

"One last moment of silence for Captain Blagg!" the preacher demanded. Everyone else in the church bowed their heads, but I kept mine up in an act of defiance for being persecuted like that.

"My head's still up," I announced bravely.

Just then, I noticed that the crowd of cowardly swabbies that I had met earlier at the funny tavern were all at church too, seated together in the front pew. The one guy who didn't have a face was especially emotional, barely able to control his weeping. "Chill out man," I called out from the back.

"Quiet!" yelled the preacher.

"The sign out front said ALL are welcome!" I said.

"Hush!" the preacher yelled.

"The Bible's fake!!!"

IV.

I Don't Like You And You Don't Like Me

After being brave at church, I hung around there for a while as everyone else from the service lingered and consoled each other about their dead friend. Everyone was really sad about this Captain Blagg guy. I didn't know the man, but people really loved him around Skalego. He must have killed a ton of whales.

The faceless swabbie from before approached me. "My friend!" he shrieked excitedly, "I thank ye for comin' to mourn in the loss of my dear stepbrother, Captain Blagg. His death has brought sorrow into the hearts of every poor soul in Skalego! Oh, cruel Lord, why'd ye take him so young!? Oh, my dear stepbrother!"

"Sorry for your loss," I was able to muster.

"Oh, why my stepbrother!? Why oh why, of all the men on Earth who could've been taken in his stead, did it have to be my dear, sweet stepbrother!?"

"My condolences," I said, instead of what I was really thinking, which was: *he was just your STEP-brother, dude.*

The faceless swabbie finally got a hold of

himself and wiped his tears away. "Well," he said, "I suppose the man died a hero's death. Is there any death more noble than one at sea?"

I was about to give him some examples of nobler ways to die, like dying saving someone's life at war or dying doing a great magic trick, but I bit my tongue and let him grieve. "Well, I'll thank ye once more for coming," he told me. "I suppose I'll return to The Drip to drown my sorrows with a small beer."

"Wait!" I cried out. "Not so fast. I have a proposition."

"Of what sort?"

"Look, I don't like *you* and *you* don't like *me*, but I'm looking to ship out on a whaling voyage. I'm going through a bit of a rough patch right now. I feel sad a lot of the time and sometimes I don't like myself, which is weird because I'm so nice. I think a couple months on the ocean and a couple dead whales under my belt is really what I need right now. I hear all the *good* sailors are already at sea, but do *you* have any interest in a nautical adventure?"

The few remnants of what was once the swabbie's face lit up like a lantern. He grabbed me by the shoulders and shook me joyfully, which I didn't appreciate. "My friend," he shrieked, "ye're speaking to just the right man, for just this very morn, my fellow swabbies and I were discussing a voyage. Please, allow me to confide in ye: there remains in my heart a small sliver of hope—small, yes, but not negligible—that contrary to what's been reported, my stepbrother Captain Blagg might not've perished after all. Ye may call it stepbrother's intuition—I still feel my sweet stepbrother's presence. It is faint, but it is there. His ship may've sunk, yes, but lesser men than he have survived worse shipwrecks! I'd like to assemble a rescue team so that we may search for him at sea. Please, let's return now to The Drip and discuss this voyage."

"Okay but try to chill out a little though."

"Aye!"

The faceless swabbie and I began the walk back to the tavern. "So, my lad," he asked me on the way, "what's yer name?"

I had to think about it for a while before I finally thought of a good name. "The name's Captain Fortnight," I told him.

"Aye! Now that's a hero's name if ever I've heard one," he told me. "My name is Kragg."

"That's fine," I said.

We arrived at The Seaman's Drip and went in there, walked past the bar to a staircase in the back corner and walked upstairs where Kragg had a room. It was a cramped little space that stunk of mold. The ceiling leaked in several places and the floorboards were soggy and rotted out. The space was furnished with nothing more than a filthy, wet mattress and an old, dimly lit oil lamp. You could tell Kragg was a bachelor. Probably because of the whole no-face thing. Plus his personality was bad.

The walls were lined with tattered old maps that Kragg had hung up, certain parts of which were circled in red ink. There was also a picture of a sexy female sailor hung which Kragg quickly ripped off the wall when I got in there. "Oh dear," he said bashfully. "Anyway," he continued, "I see, Captain, that ye've noticed my many maps. I burnt all of yesterday's evening hours trying to determine where my stepbrother Blagg's ship may've sunk, hopeless though the endeavor may seem. I have knowledge of Captain Blagg's intended course— aye, his entire itinerary—for he shared with me these details before leaving shore. Still, this knowledge is of little practical use, for at sea, what is estimated to take weeks often takes months, or then again in some cases, only days. Aye, Captain, that is why it is so daunting to determine where in this watery world I might find the remnants of my stepbrother's ship, and perhaps he himself."

"What?"

"Anyway," Kragg continued, "my fellow swabbies have offered their servitude. If I do embark on this rescue voyage, then they will gladly serve as my crew, for though they may be cowardly, their hearts swell with compassion. When they were apprised of my stepbrother's misfortune out there on the water, the details of which are still mysterious, they conceded that, indeed, Blagg may've survived, and may yet still be rescued!"

"What?"

"Captain Fortnight, we swabbies look after one another. It shall be a loyal and hearty crew serving alongside us aboard The Ted!"

"The Ted?" I asked.

"Aye! The Ted is the name of my ship! It belonged to my father. He too perished at sea only weeks ago. The ship is named eponymously—The

Ted."

The first order of business before our whaling expedition would be to change the name of the boat. *I ain't sailing on a boat named The Ted*, I thought to myself.

"Oh, what a rousing voyage it shall be out there on The Ted!" Kragg roared.

Ain't no way the boat's gonna be named The Ted, I thought.

"Oh, how powerful it makes ye feel in yer bones even just to yell out the name of the ship: The Ted!"

"Look Kragg, we're changing the name of the boat."

"Okay."

After a long discussion, Kragg and I agreed to change the name of the boat to The S.S. Captain Fortnight's Big Boat. Kragg felt a little guilty about it, but he made peace with it eventually and then we moved on to discussing more important things.

Kragg proposed that we get to work on creating a schedule for daily operations aboard The S.S. Captain Fortnight's Big Boat. "We'll need a crew member serving watch at the mast-head at all times," said Kragg, "and someone manning the helm at all hours, too." I didn't know what a "mast-head" or "helm" was and it seemed important to find out but I didn't want to ask because it always took Kragg 15 minutes to convey a very simple idea, so I looked up the words in my nautical dictionary.

Masthead /ˈmaːsthɛd/

Noun

The top of the mast; often used as a lookout point to spot hazards or whales

Helm /helm/

Noun

Wheel or tiller used to steer a ship

Contemptible Blue

What the hell is a tiller? I wondered, before we moved on to the next order of business: mapping out our route. "The sea will decide our route for us," I told Kragg, because I didn't feel like mapping out a route right now. I was a sea captain, not a cartographer. Kragg shrugged and said okay. I was getting sleepy so I dozed off while Kragg finished up the planning. I figured he needed the practice anyway, on account of him being extremely bad.

"Aye, 'tis a tremendous honor that my captain trusts me with such duties," Kragg told me. "A tremendous honor, indeed."

"Chill out Kragg," I told him.

V.

A Fine Day To Go A-Whalin'

By the time I woke up the next morning, Kragg had finished planning the voyage. He had written out a daily schedule for the crew and mapped out a route. Still, I woke up in a bad mood because my body was sore from sleeping on the floor all night. "Your tax dollars at work," I said for some reason.

I got up and drew the blinds to take in some of the warm Skalego sunlight. *'Tis a fine day to go a-whalin'*, I thought to myself, and don't you *dare* think for a *single* second that I learned the word "'tis" from Kragg because I *already* knew that word before I heard Kragg say it. If anything, *he* stole it from *me*. 'Tis one of my all-time favorite words.

The bright flash of the morning sun woke Kragg and he shot up out of bed with a big stretch and a yawn, seeming excited for our big day. "Good morning, Captain!" he roared. He was a lot to deal with so early in the morning. He went on to issue me what sounded like a dire warning: "Captain, though it may be superfluous to declare this, for a captain such as yourself must *already* know the importance of taking this precaution, don't ye forget to visit a doctor before we ship out, in order to ensure your mind and body are in good health and equipped for the voyage, for after all, when sickness comes at sea it does so violently, and the grim, peculiar combination of sickness and landlessness often gives way to ocean madness. Lord forbid, Captain, that so much as one single case of ocean madness breaks out aboard The S.S. Captain Fortnight's Big Boat. I'll be taking the same precaution myself this morning. I've an appointment in one hour's time to visit my doctor who, if all goes as well as hoped, will confirm that I am seaworthy."

"What?"

Kragg got dressed and went off to visit the town doctor. I chose to forego the doctor visit. I don't trust doctors. You can never really tell if he (or *she!!!*) knows what he's doing. After all, it was a doctor—my therapist—that talked me into becoming a whaler in the first place, which was a decision I was kind of already regretting. So far it was boring.

While Kragg went to the doctor, I hung back at his place to collect myself before our big voyage and rifle through his things a little bit. While looking through Kragg's stuff, I found a series of letters from Kragg's stepbrother, Captain Blagg. On one of the letters, Kragg had circled a passage prominently in red ink. It read: "If, my dear stepbrother, disaster strikes me and my men at sea, and if you should hear tell of my ship sinking, crashing, or otherwise meeting some cruel, peculiar fate, I urge that you do not presume me dead until you've seen, with your very own eyes, my corpse, for I've survived violent shipwrecks afore and I may yet again do the same."

"What?" I asked aloud, confused—I think Kragg's stepbrother was illiterate.

Kragg returned home from the doctor hours later and told me, "I am seaworthy, Captain Fortnight. Now then, I suppose it's time to gather the crew!"

"Okay you big fat stupid idiot."

I began to get cold feet about the whole idea. No one on the crew was going to have any nautical experience other than swabbing the deck, and the sea could be treacherous. As the saying goes: "The sea is a cruel mattress." No, wait: "The sea is a cruel *mistress*." Something like that. It's definitely something about how the sea sucks.

I tried to think positively. *At least the deck will be nice and swabbed*, I thought to myself. Whatever part of the boat the deck was, it was definitely going to be swabbed as all hell.

We walked downstairs to the bar area, where all the swabbies were already drinking. "All ye swabbies who've promised me your aid—who've expressed your willingness to ship alongside me on a voyage to search for my stepbrother—come forth now, or bear the ignominy that must be borne by any man who breaks a promise so noble!" said Kragg the drama queen. "Captain Fortnight has made the generous offer to serve as our captain—to ensure a sound and successful voyage, despite the impending storm!"

All the swabbies rose from their stools and said in unison, "A swabbie never breaks a promise! Long may we sail!"

I had my crew of men—a dozen total, including Kragg the dipshit. We all paraded down to the wharf on the far east side of town, where Kragg's dead dad's boat was moored. Kragg talked up his ship the whole way there, and I was disappointed when I finally saw it. It was a rickety old wooden craft that was all banged up from decades of use, just like my *ex-wife!* (Just a little joke to lighten things up because the book's been so serious so far.) Both of the masts were crooked, and the sails all had big holes in them, just like my *EX-WIFE* (like from before!!!). A big gust of wind came through and a couple of the sails blew right off the masts and floated away. The lifeboats were poorly secured, simply hanging from the side of the ship by a single rope. There was a sign near them that read: "DANGER! Do NOT use the lifeboats!" A couple of squatters were napping on the deck and I had to chase them off with my harpoon. Also, the ship's old crest, which read "The Ted," was still displayed proudly on the side of the ship, so I made one of my crew members paint over it before we boarded. That took a couple of hours, so while I waited, I tried to study my nautical dictionary so I'd know all the boat words before our trip, but then I accidentally dropped it in the ocean. *Well, whatever,* I thought to myself, shrugging it off. I was pretty sure sailors don't read anyway.

"The S.S. Captain Fortnight's Big Boat is loaded and she is seaworthy, Captain Fortnight," Kragg assured me.

After I finished yelling at Kragg for gendering the boat without consulting it first, we boarded our mighty vessel and prepared to lift anchor. "All aboard!" I yelled.

"We're already boarded," one of the crew members said. I fired him from the crew for being rude and then, finally, it was time to do this.

"All aboard!"

VI.

Please Don't Tell Anyone About This

Before finally hoisting our sails and leaving land behind, I called for a huddle on the quarter deck so that I could give a big rousing speech to commence our fantastic journey. The swabbies were practically foaming at the mouth when they saw how badly the deck needed to be swabbed. They couldn't *wait* to swab it. A couple of them got right to work swabbing it and I had to ask them to please wait. "Look here, stupid swabbies!" I cried. "My name is Captain Fortnight, and I think you already know why we're here: to hunt us a whale!"

"It was my understanding that we were looking for Kragg's stepbrother," one of the men said.

"Right, right, looking for Kragg's dead stepbrother," I concurred, "but also, if we happen to spot a whale or two along the way, we might as well give it a harpooning."

"Aye!" Kragg shrieked. "We'll nab every whale we can, for my stepbrother Captain Blagg would surely do the same now, if only he could. It is true, after all, that my dear stepbrother met his fate—that fate which is still uncertain—trying to hunt down Contemptible Blue."

"Contemptible Blue?" I asked.

"Aye, the contemptible blue whale!" Kragg said. "Captain Blagg spent 23 years of his life in pursuit of old Contemptible Blue! He's eluded whalers for decades. There is no bigger prize to be won at sea than he!"

This "contemptible blue" whale sounded like a hot target. If it was true that he'd eluded whalers for decades, then it didn't seem likely that *I'd* be the one to kill him, but I figured that if I was going to do this, then I was going to do it *big*. The most important thing as a captain is to believe in yourself. Also, you can't fall off the boat, or whatever. And you have to have the little captain's hat. But confidence is definitely *one* of the most important parts of being a captain.

"You leave Contemptible Blue to me!" I said proudly. "I shall nab the beast. Now then, before we set sail, if any of you are having second thoughts, speak up now! I won't have a coward on my ship!"

"Errr, Captain Fortnight," one of the men said sheepishly, "we hath confessed to thee already —my fellow swabbies and I—that we are certainly cowards. Yellow in the heart, indeed. 'Twas the very first thing we told'st thee about ourselves. I myself am terrified of fish. I am Abbadon, by the way."

"I'm afraid of thunder," another one said. "So, yes, I'll concede that I'm a bit of a coward. I am Egbert, by the way."

"I'm afraid to sleep alone. I am Wigmund," said another.

"My name is Aldous. I quit my last whaling voyage because I feared the boat was haunted," said another.

"My name is Milton. Big insecurity issues. I got kicked off my most recent voyage because I wouldn't stop asking the other sailors if they liked me," said another.

"Bartleby here. Afraid of germs," said another.

"My name is Langdon. I'm afraid of seaweed," said another. "It just feels so weird."

"My name is Norman. I'm afraid the moon is alive and that it spies on me at night," said another.

"Name's Reginald. Same fear as Norman," said another.

Welp, this doesn't sound promising, I thought to myself, but alas, it was all I had. "You'll have to do," I told the men. "Now, let's go hunt us a whale!"

Contemptible Blue

"Yeah! And find Kragg's stepbrother!" someone yelled.

"Whatever," I said.

"Captain, I shall raise the anchor and hoist our sails now," Kragg said. "Will ye man the helm?"

"You know what, can you take this one? I actually just manned a helm yesterday and I'm a little helmed out," I said, having no idea what Kragg had just asked me to do. He obliged. He had been taking some sailing classes at night school and was glad to take the reins on this one. "Don't fuck up!" I told him.

Minutes later, with our sails hoisted high and proudly in the sky, and with Kragg at the helm, we were officially cruising merrily atop the open ocean. I wondered which ocean it was, but it seemed too late to ask.

Soon, the shore became but a distant speck

in our rear view. As I watched the land shrink and finally disappear behind us, I felt a throb of excitement in my gut. "We're really doin' this thing!" I said aloud.

"Yeah!" one of my enthusiastic crew members yelled back.

"Shut up!" I said back, because I was trying to have a *private* moment.

As we cruised on, with the brisk, salty sea air flowing through my hair, bathed in the hot yellow sunlight of summer, I remained vigilant, keeping my eyes on the water and looking out for any signs of whale activity. The sea was calm, but I wasn't spotting so much as a single fish. I guess news had spread around the ocean that there was a *new* whaling crew in town, and all the stupid whales knew that it was wise to lie low. "Hide all you want," I yelled at the ocean, "but you can't hide forever!"

"Yeah, thou can't hide forever!" echoed one

of my crewmen.

"Shut up!"

A few minutes later, Kragg finally emerged from the bridge where he'd been manning the helm and he joined me outside on the main deck. "Ahoy!" he said, trying way too hard to sound like a nautical guy. "Captain Fortnight, yer eyes beam vigilant as ye watch the water. Now *that,* my friend, is the way of the whaler. Nothing escapes yer watch, aye? Tell me, Captain: what is it that ye find so seductive about the whaling life?"

"Well, I read a few pages of *Moby Dick,* and I guess the idea of conquering something as powerful as a whale really spoke to me," I told him.

Kragg laughed heartily and nodded, taking a big puff off his pipe. "I understand," he said. "Some men may tell ye yer compulsions are morbid, overzealous—that they are perhaps symptoms of a restless heart—but I myself believe that yer feelings are the natural ones of the truly venerable man. Though I myself—an ordinary seaman of ill repute, little experience and depletable courage—have not felt the euphoric rush of sinking a harpoon in the flesh of the mighty blue whale, I've spent idle hours musing about such victories, and I can only dream, Captain Fortnight, that these victories must make one feel akin to God."

"*Right?*" I said.

"Aye."

"Hey Kragg?"

"Yes?"

"Do you ever feel like... I don't know, like you were destined for greater things than a life on land could afford you?"

"Aye. I believe that is the suspicion of every sailor."

"Right? It's like, there's no *magic* on land. All the magic is here at sea, and I deserve my cut of it. And as long as I put my mind to it, nothing can stop me from grabbing it."

"Ah, ye're one of a quixotic sort, aye Captain?"

"Definitely," I said, assuming that "quixotic" was a synonym for "good."

"I do believe yer dreams'll come true out here, Captain."

"Wow. It feels good to talk about this stuff. Thanks Kragg."

"The pleasure is all mine."

"This was nice."

"Aye."

"Hey Kragg?"

"Yes?"

"Don't tell anyone about this."

"Pardon?"

"Please don't tell the other crew members that we had this talk."

"All right."

"Only because—you know—you're a lowly swabbie, and I'm a big time sea captain."

"Right."

"And I can't have my crew thinking you and I are, like, *friends.*"

"All right."

"It just makes me look bad, is all."

"All right."

"You get it though, right? Like, I'm not being an asshole?"

"No, no. It's all right."

"Okay, cool. So just so we're clear: this was a nice talk, *but...*"

"I shan't tell a soul that you and I shared this lovely moment with one another."

"Okay, cool. Because—and I *swear* I'm not trying to be an asshole here—if you tell anyone, I'll be so pissed off."

"Understood, Captain."

"And I would have to come after you, or

whatever."

"All right."

"Maybe shoot you with my harpoon, I don't know."

"I understand."

"...Throw you off the boat, or whatever."

"I understand."

"Cool. Thanks Kragg."

"All right."

"Cool."

I noticed that some of the swabbies were watching me talk to Kragg and I didn't want them to think that I had sunk down to their level socially so in order to set an example I pulled Kragg's pants down and I pointed at his penis and I said, "¡Ay, caramba, that's a small penis, mi amigo!" Kragg actually had a huge dick so it wasn't a good slam, but I think it got the message across.

The rest of the day passed with not much action. If I'm being honest, that first day out there was underwhelming. I'd expected more of an adventure. A daring whale chase, perhaps. A legendary pirate battle. Some sort of mutiny. Maybe even some swashbuckling, whatever that is. But all we did was sail peacefully across the ocean in a boat. I didn't swashbuckle *once*, as far as I know.

As the sun began to set and the air grew cold, we retired to our quarters to sleep for the night. Reginald, my crew member who was afraid of the moon, was scheduled to serve watch at the mast-head, which, as it turns out, is a spot at the top of a mast that's often used as a lookout point to spot hazards or whales. I'm not sure why my nautical dictionary had so much trouble describing it. Reginald was pretty spooked out because he was slightly closer to the moon up there in the big, tall mast-head, but he was managing alright. "Don't fuck up!" I advised him before I went off to bed, because it's important for a captain to be a mentor.

I decided to do some light reading before going to bed—*that's* how bored I was. I thumbed through my pages of *Moby Dick* for a few minutes, not really "absorbing" it, before finally giving up and lying down to sleep. *I BETTER swashbuckle tomorrow,* I thought to myself.

VII.

Downtime & Good Omens

Over the next few weeks, I came to an unfortunate realization: *most* time spent at sea is downtime. It wasn't quite the thrill I was expecting. We didn't spot a single whale. Instead, we continued to cruise briskly across a calm and unsurprising ocean for weeks and weeks waiting for something to happen. I was, essentially, just floating around on water with several sad, single, broken men who seemed prone for death. I could have crashed the swimming pool at a senior living center and gotten the same effect.

My crew kept busy. Kragg manned the helm and steered us along while the swabbies swabbed and took turns manning the mast-head. I didn't really have many captain duties to worry about so I tried to take up a hobby to keep myself busy. A couple of the guys on my crew were big into whittling, so I tried to get into it too, but I couldn't get the hang of it. It's probably something you have to learn when you're young or else you never get it. I think whittling is a young man's game.

I read a little more *Moby Dick* to see what the main guy Ishmael did to stay busy, but it seemed like he spent most of his downtime writing *Moby Dick.* Imagine being so bored you write a whaling novel out of spite.

I frequently thought about jumping ship

and swimming back to shore and just commissioning a professional whaler to kill a whale *for* me, but I wasn't confident that that would scratch the itch. *I* had to do it, and I had to accept that nabbing my whale was going to take a lot longer than I'd expected. I had originally thought that this whaling adventure would take, at the absolute most, 12 hours. I didn't even lock my house or get a babysitter or shut my oven off before leaving.

Things started to heat up when, finally, we discovered a big ship full of dead guys. "Now *this* I could get used to!" I yelled excitedly. "We got a ship full o' dead guys, boys!"

We spotted it floating aimlessly there in the ocean with her sails at half mast. "These idiots don't even know how to raise the sails all the way!" I said to Kragg with a big laugh, then explained that there's a lot of reasons that a sailor might intentionally fly their sails at half mast. He really sucked the joy out of everything. "Whaling is supposed to be *fun*," I reminded him sternly.

We boarded the competing ship to discover the whole crew dead in a pile on the main deck. "Looks like someone better swab *this* deck," I joked to my crew. Then they started actually swabbing it, because they couldn't tell I was joking. I let them just do it while I raided the ship for supplies.

I was able to find some useful items. I snatched a crate full of harpoons for hunting, some foodstuffs for eating and the dead captain's personal diary for entertainment. I flipped through it a bit and found some of his writing about being on the hunt for Contemptible Blue and fearing for his life out there. He wrote about some sort of disease outbreak on his ship and about fearing a violent mutiny. I guess they were ideas for a short story or something. I wished he'd written about his *actual* journey out there, because it would have been pretty cool to find out how he and his crew died.

After raiding the ship we moved on, and a few hours later we passed the wreckage of another whaleship that looked like it had been bitten in half by some large creature. The next day, we cruised past the wreckage of yet another ship in the same condition. Discovering all those ravaged whaleships full of dead sailors was reassuring— our competition was weak.

VIII.
Harpoon-Man

Then one morning I woke up in my stateroom to the faint sound of music being played outside on the foredeck. I ran up there to discover that all ten of my crew members had found some musical instruments, which originally belonged to

Kragg's dad, and they were playing a sea shanty together. They sounded *killer.* Kragg pumped a beautiful melody on a concertina and Wigmund, Aldous and Egbert banged away on the skins. We had Abbadon on the fife, and Milton and Reginald were shredding on fiddles. Motherfuckin' Langdon and Norman were hammerin' out some juicy banjo riffs, and my man Bartleby took care of the low-end, fing'rin' out a positively *infectious* upright bass line. I joined in too, providing some hand claps for percussion and crooning some lead vocals. I wrote some *sick* lyrics, too:

> *"Throw away the stowaway*
> *Throw him out to sea*
> *For no free rides and no free shelter*
> *Have we got for he"*

We jammed for hours, ripping through some classic sea shanties of old and improvising a few more originals of our own. No one played a single sour note. Absolutely *killer.* Finally, after a particularly groovy, 14 minute-long improvised sea shanty about mermaids, we all took a cheeky bow, laughed and exchanged hugs. "Hell yeah!" I yelled out. "Now *that's* how you play a sea shanty, *baby!*"

Abbadon, our fife player, laughed a joyous laugh and said, "I concur! I came upon these musical instruments stashed away in the cargo hold this morn. Oh, what a sad sight it was, seeing them stashed away and neglected in the dark, dingy cargo hold, when in fact there is no more joyous way to pass the idle hours at sea than to sing sea shanties!"

"Hell yeah, my man!" I said. "*Fuck* yeah. Alright, let's run through 'Throw Away The Stowaway' one more time. Everybody ready? A-one, a-two, a-one, two, three, four!"

Just as we were about to play, some sudden, jolting force struck The S.S. Captain Fortnight's Big Boat from below, rocking the entire ship and sending us falling to the floor. "What on

Earth was that?" one of the crew members cried.

"Something big," Kragg said dramatically, because everything always had to be a big *production* with him.

We all rushed to the port side with harpoons in hand and leaned over the bulwark, peering down into the water below. That's when I finally spotted my prey after weeks of waiting. The faint silhouette of the mighty blue whale lurked just below the surface of the water, swimming alongside the boat. "Ho! 'Tis a leviathanic blue whale!" cried Langdon, the crew member with the seaweed phobia. I could tell he was really proud of himself for using "leviathanic" like that, so to take him down a peg I said, "Whatever, seaweed boy!" He was bummed.

"Good lord, could it be... Contemptible Blue?" Kragg spoke in a whisper.

"Pardon me, Captain, but that creature is not a wha—" Abbadon the fife player began to say.

Contemptible Blue

"To the whaleboats!" Kragg shouted.

"To hell with the damn whaleboats!" I yelled, even though it was a good idea to use the whaleboats. It just felt appropriate to say. *To hell with the damn whaleboats, mi amigo!*

The whale began to thrash violently as he swam along, twisting and turning and slapping his tail against the water. He seemed to be in a panic. "Rightfully so, thy awful whale!" I yelled, then my crew looked at me funny, I think maybe because I used "thy" incorrectly. "Oh, sorry I don't speak in *slang,*" I yelled at them angrily. "Some of us are *educated.*"

I steadied myself up against the bulwark and I cocked back my harpoon, ready to hurl it. The adrenaline was coursing through my veins, making me feel superhuman. Like a superhuman whose superpower was that he owned a harpoon. "Harpoon-Man," perhaps.

I chucked my weapon at the mighty,

thrashing whale, missing him by about six feet. I really should have been practicing my harpoon skills during those preceding weeks, but I'd been too busy trying to learn to whittle, and then later working hard to impose a ban on whittling aboard the ship because it wasn't fair that I was the only one who couldn't whittle.

The splash scared the whale off and he plunged deeper down, his silhouette disappearing into the abyss. The crew breathed a collective, sad sigh. We all just sort of stood there, feeling disappointed and not knowing what to say.

"I pawned my wedding ring for that harpoon," I said, trying to break the glum silence with a funny anecdote.

"We should have used the whaleboats," said Norman, the crew member who was afraid of the moon.

"Hey, fuck you, Norman. Why don't you go hide from the moon?" I said.

"Hey, fuck *you*," Norman said.

"Fuck you."

"Fuck you!"

"Shut up Norman."

"Fuck you."

"You know what, dude? Fuck you."

"Well, fuck you."

"Are you tryin' to catch the hands or what, motherfucker? Fuck off."

"*You* fuck off."

"You're the one who should fuck off actually."

"No, *you're* the one who should."

"Um, actually, no—*you're* the one who should."

"Fuck off."

"Actually, *you* fuck off."

Everyone was in low spirits after the failed attempt to hunt that whale. Personally, I blamed Kragg, somehow. I tried to raise everyone's spirit by getting another sea shanty jam going. "You guys wanna shred a little bit?" I proposed, but the crew seemed like they were kind of "done" with sea shanty practice for the day. They all scampered off and got back to their work duties. I was disappointed, because I was way more interested in the band than the whaling at this point.

"Good practice today, guys," I called out to them as they went. "We sound wicked. We'll re-group tonight and run through those tunes again. When we get back to shore, we definitely gotta try to book some gigs. Maybe set up a little mini-tour, hit up all the taverns. I think we really got somethin' here."

Kragg hung back to try and console me. "There are plenty of whales in the sea," he said while giving me a pat on the back, even though it was against ship rules to touch me. Just as I began to retreat to my quarters and Kragg began to retreat to the bridge, we heard a splashing down in the water on our port side again. We peered over the bulwark to discover that our elusive whale had reemerged. He was floating on his back and flailing his fins wildly, looking kind of queasy. Finally, he opened his mouth, made some awful, gurgling sound, and then hocked up an entire human being out of his throat and into the water. I had seen plenty of human beings get *eaten* by *plenty* of different animals in my time (I managed a zoo for a few years and did a bad job), but never someone getting puked back up like that. "Sick!" I yelled. Looking revitalized, the whale submerged quickly back into the deep and disappeared.

The puked-up man was limp and chewed to shreds, but appeared to be conscious. "Good heavens!" Kragg yelled. "That man is alive! To the life preservers!"

"To hell with the damn life preservers!" I yelled for some reason.

"Captain Fortnight, I—"

"Okay, fine—to the life preservers!"

IX.

First Aid

"This was a pretty good idea that I had, to use the life preservers, huh Kragg?" I said to Kragg as we tossed the life preserver overboard and into the water below. "Yes Captain," he agreed halfheartedly.

The mystery man bobbing in the waves below grabbed for the life preserver and Kragg and I pulled him up onto the foredeck. I did most of the work, not Kragg. The mystery man, covered in stomach slime, sprawled limply out on the deck, shivering from the cold. I noticed that one of his feet had been chewed clean off his ankle. "Laddie," Kragg said to the man, "it would seem ye're in the Lord's good graces, for ye've been swallowed whole by a whale and yet here ye are now, alive to live another day!"

"That was a dolphin," the impish man murmured weakly in a British accent, still spitting up ocean water.

"Huh?" Kragg asked.

"That was a dolphin, not a whale," he said.

Kragg and I, both blushing, looked at each feeling embarassed. "Psst," I whispered to Kragg, "can neither one of us tell the difference between a whale and a dolphin?"

"I suppose not," Kragg said sadly, looking down at his feet. "Wow, this is humiliating," he admitted.

"Please," the mystery man said, "have you got a first aid kit on this ship? And perhaps a spare cabin in which to sleep? I'm a doctor. I can fix myself up, if only I had the tools. Please, I've been lost at sea for weeks. I had to eat my own foot!"

"You know what? This freaking rules," I said aloud, excited that this nautical adventure was finally getting interesting. "Can we just take a minute to appreciate this?"

Kragg immediately rushed to the man's aid, probably because he was so desperate to be liked. He flung him over his shoulder, carried him down into the forehold and brought him into one of the spare cabins and then retrieved the first aid kit for him. The rest of the crew gathered around to watch, all looking a little alarmed. "Nothing to see here, folks!" I told the crew. "Just some puked up British guy who ate his own foot."

The doctor asked to be left alone so he could bandage up his wounds. Kragg called for a "crew meeting" in the meantime, which pissed me off because I was pretty sure only *I* had the authority to call a crew meeting, so I told Kragg that I was putting two "points" on his "record" as punishment. I hadn't worked out exactly how the disciplinary "points" system worked yet, but I assured Kragg that it was bad to have two points.

"Aww man," he said sadly.

X.

Your Worst Night-Maritime

The whole S.S. Captain Fortnight's Big Boat crew moved to my stateroom to talk about the events of the day. "This is where the magic happens!" I joked to my crew as I let them in my room, then showed them my magic kid I'd brought from home. "Pretty cool," they agreed.

"My braves," Kragg began, "we've got matters to discuss. Aye, something dire."

"I think I know what you're gonna say: we should get a second fife player in the band," I said. "I'm glad you said that—I was thinking the same thing. Well, I guess when we get back to shore we can set up some auditions. I got a buddy that works at a music school who can help us find someone. Also, I've been thinking about band names. What about 'Your Worst Night-Maritime'? It's like 'your worst nightmare' but with 'maritime,' because of how we're ocean guys."

"The matter at hand that troubles me so deeply relates in no way to our recreational playing of music, nor has the thought of recruiting an additional fife player crossed my mind," Kragg said. "Let us discuss our new passenger, the doctor who was swallowed whole and spat up by the very same dolphin we tried to hunt today. Err, I mean 'whale.' The *whale* we tried to hunt today."

"Kragg can't tell whales and dolphins apart!!!" I blurted out.

"Come on man!" Kragg pleaded.

Kragg went on to explain that we needed to be wary of our new passenger, in case he had gone mad after being lost at sea for so long. Plus, cannibalistic savages from exotic lands were sometimes known to stow away on whaling ships and feast upon the crew members. We couldn't be too careful with this guy. *I* managed to inherit an expensive boat and become a sea captain without ever having been on a boat before, plus I hadn't heard of whaling until a few weeks ago, so *this* guy could be *anyone.*

Kragg went on to propose that we host a crew dinner next day and invite the passenger to dine with us so that we could gently interrogate him and make sure he wasn't a threat. "Cool," I agreed. "So, getting back on track here: are we all cool with the name 'Your Worst Night-Maritime'?" I asked. The crew just looked down at their feet, not saying anything for a little while. "That's pretty good," Abbadon finally conceded.

"Right on!" I said. I was excited to hurry up and finish this whaling trip so we could get back to shore and play some shows. Music is my life.

XI.

My Behemoth, My Bane, My Contemptible Blue

Tensions were high on The S.S. Captain Fortnight's Big Boat and no one felt great. Kragg had everyone nervous about our strange new passenger, and I personally felt extremely unconfident after my failed attempt to kill that "whale" earlier. I had to face a harsh reality: I was unprepared for the whaling life, and it was time to learn all that I needed to learn in order to carry on. I needed to study up.

I climbed the ladder down into the forehold and went to Kragg's cabin to borrow some of his whale books. Kragg had turned his cabin into a mini-library, stocked full of nautical encyclopedias. I didn't have much respect for Kragg, but I guess it was cool that he was taking charge of his education like that. When I entered his quarters, he was sprawled out in his bed reading a self-help book geared towards sailors called *Releasing The Inner Seaman In You.* "Ha ha ha," I said, pointing at the funny book. Then I said, "Alright, enough joking around, Kragg. I need to get serious about whaling. I'm here for some of your whale books. I need to cram."

"I am happy to share my literature, Captain!" Kragg said. "Please, my friend, help yerself to anything that catches yer eye!"

"Okay but chill out a little bit Kragg," I insisted.

The walls of Kragg's cabin were lined with scrawled-upon maps, just like his home back in Skalego. He'd also hung two oil paintings: one of his dead dad, Captain Ted, and one of his dead stepbrother, Captain Blagg. He had some candles lit underneath each painting in their honor. I advised him it was a fire hazard and for the safety of the crew I made him blow out the candles and throw the paintings overboard.

Kragg's book collection was massive. I guess he was a pretty materialistic person. I browsed his selection and took all the books I could find that had a whale on the cover. "It's gonna take forever to read these," I moaned.

"Ha ha ha!" Kragg bellowed. "I suppose so, Captain, for even if every tree on the Lord's green Earth was chopped down, chippered, pulped and turned to paper, ye'd exhaust the supply writing all there is to be said about the curious nature of the whale, and about the brave men who hunt them."

"What?"

"Anyway," Kragg continued, "I'd be glad to help ye study, Captain, for I too have much to learn. May you and I pledge to never mistake a dolphin for a whale again."

"You'd really help me study?" I asked Kragg.

"It would be my tremendous pleasure," Kragg said.

"Wow. Thanks Kragg."

"Ye're welcome."

"I appreciate that."

"'Tis really no trouble."

"Hey Kragg?"

"Aye?"

"Don't tell anyone about us hanging out like this."

"I shan't."

"Because you're a dirty, stupid, pathetic, smelly deck swabber and—"

"I remember, yes. Ye can't have the other crew members thinkin' we're chums."

"Exactly."

"No problem."

"Cool. Thanks for understanding, Kragg."

"All right."

"It's just... I really need the crew to think I'm strong, you know? And cool."

"I understand. For what it's worth—though

I imagine my lowly opinion is of little worth to a man of your repute—I consider ye a strong captain, if not merely a trusted ally."

"And the second thing?"

"Pardon?"

"The other part..."

"Oh, yes. I think that too."

"Could you say it though?"

"I think ye're cool."

"Thanks Kragg."

Kragg and I got to work looking through some of his whaling books together, then I noticed that one of them was a coloring book called *Let's Color Whales* and Kragg had only completed half of it, so we kind of got caught up in finishing it. Kragg and I colored late into the night, pouring ourselves into our studies, and by about 2 A.M. we had colored all the whales. We didn't learn much, but it was a nice way to unwind after a tough day, so it was time well spent. We colored all the whales.

After we finished *Let's Color Whales*, Kragg quizzed me on what the different parts of the boat were called with flashcards, so that I could better direct the crew aboard The S.S. Captain Fortnight's Big Boat. I had sort of been letting Kragg run the day-to-day operations the previous few weeks, and even though I had done a lot of great work as captain (passing that whittling ban, making Kragg throw out his dangerous paintings of beloved dead relatives, frontmanning Your Worst Night-Maritime, etc.) it was time to get even more involved.

As a way of saying thanks to Kragg for helping me, I took those two points off his record. He confessed to me that those two points had really been weighing on his conscience. "I couldn't sleep," he admitted.

Wigmund, the crew member who was afraid to sleep alone, interrupted our study session to ask Kragg if he could sleep in his cabin. Kragg obliged. "Goodnight, pathetic swabbies," I told Kragg and Wigmund as I saw myself out.

"Goodnight," said Kragg. "May the Lord bless ye with a restful slumber."

"Uh, well, actually, I'm an athei—" I began to say, but Kragg and Wigmund had already fallen asleep. *I'll tell them tomorrow*, I decided, then retreated back to my stateroom.

"What a perilous day," I said to myself—I was practicing speaking how the other sailors spoke. "'Twas most pathetic, my attempt at hunting that dolphin today, but tomorrow I shall wake more prepared, and I shall conquer my behemoth, my bane, my Contemptible Blue, and return to shore a hero, shrouded in glory and honor," I said. I got into bed and jerked off my penis a little bit and then went to sleep.

Contemptible Blue

XII.

Slaughter on The Ted

The next evening, Kragg prepared an early dinner and we all gathered in his cabin to dine and interrogate our new passenger. "Hark!" said Kragg, just making up words at this point. "Thank ye, my friends, for yer company! And let us welcome our new passenger."

We all turned to look at the doctor, who had stitched up his various wounds and fixed himself up with a pegleg, probably just to rub it in our faces that he was a doctor. He seemed to be in a daze. He glanced around the cabin, looking awestruck. "Oh dear," he finally said, "it's all washing over me. I was too much in a fog to realize it yesterday when you fished me from the ocean, but... this ship is called The Ted, is it not?"

"No," I said.

"Yes!" Kragg squealed. "But how could

ye've known such a thing, unless ye'd spent some time on this very ship, or at the very least, my friend, were friendly with the late Captain Ted, who perished at sea only just weeks ago?"

"It's actually called The S.S. Captain Fortnight's Boa—" I began to explain.

"Oh, heavens," the doctor interrupted. "It's a small world, gents. It really is a small, small world. Gentlemen, my name is Dr. Moseley. I specialize in nautical disease, for I was a captain myself before studying medicine in London. I served as a crew member on *this* very ship, only weeks ago. I was invited along by Captain Ted, with promises of handsome compensation, to keep Captain Ted's crew in proper health."

Kragg's eyes began to well up with tears, even though I had banned crying on the boat. "Captain Ted was my father," he spoke. "This craft is named after the man."

"No it's not," I clarified.

"Kragg, has it been told to you, or to the loved ones of the previous crew that once manned this ship, how Captain Ted and his men met their fate?" asked Dr. Moseley.

"Nay, Dr. Moseley, 'tis a mystery to me. I was told simply—and rather cavalierly—by some member of a competing crew who claimed to've heard secondhandedly, that my father's ship was spotted floating aimlessly and seemingly uncaptained by some fellow whalers, and upon an investigation of the ship by these men, my father and his crew were found dead and bloodied."

"Your father," Dr. Moseley explained, "fell violently ill with quite the grim cocktail of nautical diseases, which ravaged both his body and his mind. The Lord seems to have had a grudge with that man, grand as he was."

"Actually, I'm an *athei*—" I began to say, contributing to the conversation.

"I diagnosed Captain Ted and warned that

he should be quarantined temporarily while I did my best to treat him," Dr. Moseley continued, "but he rejected my diagnosis, telling me he had not the time for distractions—not with his hunt for Contemptible Blue underway. I'm certain that *you* —a learned sailor—is aware that nautical illness often develops into ocean madness. I suppose that that's what happened to your poor, unfortunate father. I believe, Kragg, that it wasn't disease of the body that did him in, but ultimately, disease of the mind. He tossed me overboard and left me to drown. I'm not sure how much later it was that Captain Ted and his men died on this ship. All I know, Kragg, is that I was splashing around out at sea for weeks before that bloody dolphin swallowed me up."

"Listen buddy," I butted in, "enough pleasantries. Let's get down to business: are you a vicious cannibal savage?"

"What? No," Dr. Moseley said. "Did you

not just listen to my story?" he asked. I hadn't.

"Aye!" interrupted Kragg. "How unfathomable are the odds, Doctor, that ye were fished up and sheltered on the very same ship from which ye were tossed only weeks ago?"

"It is more than just a *wee* miracle, innit?" the doctor said, rubbing it in our faces that he was British. "Furthermore," he continued, "if I may be uncompromisingly truthful—and I do not wish to raise alarm—but I feel a dark cloud over this ship. It is true, after all, that the previous owner and captain of this ship, before it was purchased and captained by Captain Ted, fell to sea madness as well, as did his predecessor, and *his* predecessor, and *his* predecessor, too. Ghastly misfortune seems to befall all who captain this ship."

The whole crew turned and looked at me, looking concerned. "Wait, *what's* up?" I asked, because I hadn't been paying attention for a while.

"Captain Fortnight," Kragg said, "how are

ye feelin'? Are ye confident that ye're of a sound mind, and will remain as such for the remainder of this voyage?"

"Yeah sure. Anyway, fellas," I said, trying to change the subject to something actually interesting, "I've got a new shanty that I've been playing around with, and I think it has lead single potential. It's called 'I'll Be Your Life Preserver.' It's kind of inspired by a girl I used to know. So it's a simple I V vi IV chord progression, and for drums I'm thinking we could maybe bring in a tambourine player to—"

"Let us eat!" Kragg insisted.

The crew dug into the fresh cod that Kragg had prepared for dinner, while I just kind of mashed mine around with a fork, making a sour face. I don't like fish. "Kragg, I don't like fish," I proclaimed. He ignored me. I was feeling left out.

The crew finished their cod and all leaned back in their chairs contentedly, their bellies full, while Kragg and Dr. Moseley continued to talk more about their adventures at sea. The doctor shared some stories about other horrific things he had seen as a nautical doctor, and Kragg shared some funny things that had happened to him while he was swabbing the deck. Really just a lot of stories about him accidentally dropping his broom. "Ye should've seen it," he'd insist.

Kragg and Dr. Moseley seemed to get along really well, and *don't* you *dare* think for *one* minute that I was jealous about the doctor becoming Kragg's new best friend because I *didn't* care at all and I *didn't* even like Kragg, so it was fine. *Good for them,* I thought to myself. It didn't even bother me. Kragg sucked.

Kragg and the stupid friend-stealing British dweeb Dr. Moseley excused themselves to go share a smoke from Kragg's pipe and I *wasn't* jealous that Kragg didn't invite me to come smoke with them. Not even a little bit at all. Kragg is lame and he stinks like shit and he's fat and he sucks, so whatever.

The rest of the crew and I lingered back at the dinner table, just kind of sitting there quietly and uncomfortably, looking down at our laps. Kragg was kind of the glue that held the crew together socially, and it was a little awkward without him there to make conversation. "Do you guys want to talk about girls?" someone suggested, which was met with shrugs.

"Just go swab the deck," I finally told the crew. They all jumped up excitedly and rushed to the deck. "Let's do this thing!" one of them yelled.

After hearing about the tragedy that befell, which is a real word, Kragg's dad's crew, my guys were feeling uneasy. Shortly after dinner, Kragg the backstabber told me, "Captain Fortnight, at a time like this, when it feels as if the dark, dense clouds of misfortune hang over our vessel, I believe the crew needs to hear the reassuring words of a virtuous captain. Perhaps a speech is in order, to issue yer advice on how best to carry on."

In order to demonstrate my value as a strong captain, I climbed all the way up the mizzenmast to deliver a reassuring speech from on high. Then I accidentally slipped off the mizzenmast and got tangled up in the rigging. "Ahh! I'm tangled up in the rigging!" I yelled. I wiggled my way out and fell back down onto the deck and landed in a crate of spare harpoons. "Yowch! I fell in a spare crate of harpoons!" I yelled. I plucked the harpoons out and went to go finish my speech but then an albatross swooped down and pecked me a bunch. "Ow ow ow, a albatross pecked me a bunch!" I shrieked. I accidentally stepped on the end of spare anchor that was standing there and it flew back and conked me on the head and I went flying off the side of the ship. "Oh no! That anchor conked me!" I yelled as I fell overboard and splashed into a floating pile of whale shit. "I fell in shit!" I yelled. The crew threw me a life preserver and I climbed back up and finished my big speech on how to carry forward in dark times: "I guess just, like, try not to fuck up or anything," I proclaimed wisely. The crew nodded unenthusiastically and then kind of just wandered off, looking nervous.

I got the strange, inexplicable sense that my crew didn't quite trust me as a leader. That night, I promised myself that I would turn things around and rise to the occasion, but in the days that followed, those "dark clouds" that Dr. Moseley the virgin had alluded to seemed to dawn on me when a strange series of losses and misfortunes began to unfold and things began to fall apart for me in ways that I didn't expect and definitely didn't deserve.[1]

---

1   I'm nice

Contemptible Blue

XIII.

Milton Died

That same night I began to feel woozy, and not just because I skipped dinner. Something wasn't right. I felt a strange soreness in my arms and legs, and my skin was getting itchy. I almost considered consulting Dr. Moseley, but I didn't quite trust him. For all I knew, he still might have been one of those cannibal savages. Sure, he was well spoken, and after dinner he showed me his medical degree from the University of London, but lying about being a UoL graduate is *exactly* how *I* got a job as a doctor years back for a few days in order to make a quick buck to pay off some horsefighting debts. Anyways...

I tried to sleep the sickness off, but I began to feel feverish and couldn't get a single wink of rest. I noticed a big, gruesome rash developing on my body, right next to all my preexisting rashes. I tossed and turned all night until sunrise. Fortunately, Kragg cheered me up that next morning when he came into my stateroom and told me one of my crew members had committed suicide—that really put things into perspective for me and reminded me that things could always be worse. "Wow, thanks man," I told Kragg.

Kragg was bawling his eyes out when he told me the bad news. He tried to hug me and I had to reject him because captains aren't allowed to hug, I don't think. I also had to remind him about the crying ban.

"It's all right to cry," he sniffled. Then he explained that Milton, the insecure crew member of mine who had gotten kicked off his previous whaling voyage because he wouldn't stop asking the other sailors if they liked him, had jumped overboard last night. Kragg, his hands trembling, handed me the note that Milton left behind. In it, Milton explained that he felt like none of the other crew members thought he was cool, so he was going to jump off the boat. "Wow, that guy was really insecure," I said to Kragg.

"'Twas Milton's one and only weakness!" Kragg shrieked.

"Well, he was also a bad sailor, so it was *one* of his weaknesses, for sure," I said.

Things felt even grimmer now on The S.S. Captain Fortnight's Big Boat. The whole crew wept aloud, hugging one another while cursing at the sky. "Why Milton!?" one of them shrieked. "The gentlest and most compassionate soul I've ever known in all my miserable years! Oh, if only we'd told him he was cool!"

"Oh, Milton, why?!?" Kragg yelled, making the whole thing about him. It was an uncomfortable scene. I guess I didn't think death would be this big of a deal on a whaling ship. You have to figure that, on a typical whaling voyage, *most* of the guys die. I honestly couldn't believe it took so long for someone to die. I had fifty bucks on Kragg dying three weeks ago in my crew dead pool.

I began to worry how Your Worst Night-Maritime would fare without our lead fiddle player. Maybe the savage played fiddle.

I felt like I had to get away from it all so I retreated to my stateroom and drew a picture of a whale and hung it on my wall and threw darts at it, still feeling sick. In my absence, my crew members turned to Dr. Moseley, the possible savage, for support. They seemed to love the guy. Personally, I didn't see why everyone thought he was so smart. How many smart people do you know who've eaten their own foot? Other than my life coach I couldn't name a single one. Maybe it was the British accent that had my crew fooled. I thought maybe it would help my standing with the crew if I had a British accent too, so I practiced one in my stateroom, but it kept coming out more Norwegian than British, and I couldn't remember if Norwegians were good or not.

I heard a knock at my door. It was Dr. Moseley. "Out of my stateroom, cannibal!" I insisted. "Get back, savage!"

"Oi, Fortnight! I am a former sea captain and a renowned doctor of medicine from England with a home and a family. I'm not a savage and certainly not a bloody cannibal."

"Tell that to your *foot*," I shot back. It was a good slam. If you're ever in that situation—where a guy who ate his own foot is trying to convince you he's not a cannibal—you can use that. You have to credit me though.

"I'm only here to make sure you're feeling all right, mate," the doctor insisted. "How are you recovering after the news of Milton's suicide?"

"Who?" I asked, because I had forgotten about the Milton stuff.

"Your mate Kragg is a wreck," Dr. Moseley

continued. "He's lost a lot of people near and dear to his heart recently—his father, Milton, his stepbrother. The poor bloke has even gone and convinced himself his stepbrother is still alive out there. Captain, you don't look so well yourself, mate. How are you feeling?"

"Like a million bucks!" I said, before excusing myself to go diarrhea off the side of the boat.

After finishing up the aforementioned diarrhea, I noticed that three of my crew members were fishing off the side of the deck with fishing poles. It looked fun. I went and joined them, then realized that they hadn't actually cast their lures and that they were just standing there holding poles pretending to fish. I kept forgetting how stupid they were. Then I noticed that Abbadon, my crew member who had a phobia of fish, was off by himself, lowering one of the whaleboats into the water.

Contemptible Blue

"Whale ho?" I asked Abbadon.

"Nay, Captain," he replied. "Thou need not man thy harpoon and prepare for a hunt. Nay, Captain, for I lowereth this whaleboat not for a whale, but for my own selfish escape. I am sorry, Captain."

"Huh?" I asked.

"Oh, my friend, my captain," said Abbadon, his eyes beginning to well up with tears, "thou wilt think me a coward, most certainly, but I must abandon this voyage. I am boarding this whaleboat and returning to shore whence I came. I shall retreat to dry land—so far inland that the waves can not be heard, for I admit now, Captain, that I wast made not for the sea."

"Is it because of the fish thing?" I asked.

"Yes," Abbadon said, sounding ashamed. "Oh, what sort of sailor am I, afraid of fish? I am no sailor at all. No, no, just merely a simple land lubber. I dreamed I might conquer my fears this voyage, once and for all, but I confess now, my heart as heavy as all the sea itself, that I am simply no seaman. I must go. And if thou art a man who cherishes his own life, and the lives of his noble crew, too, then thou too shalt do the same, Captain Fortnight, or else that contemptible blue whale— that awful, blue leviathan—will bring destruction to thy craft, and indeed, thine entire crew. And to thineself, of course. Certainly thou hast heard the tales already, one-thousand times over, of old Contemptible Blue. He is the Devil. I know thou doth not fear the Lord, nor the Devil, nor even Mother Earth with all her awful tricks, but should Contemptible Blue cross thy path—should thy modest vessel come near enough to the beast to stare him in the eyes—then finally, thou *shalt* behold his power, when thou seeth the Devil in his eyes."

"Listen, Abbadon," I said, "I'm going to be honest: I have no idea what you just said. Straight up, I did not understand a word of it. Literally I don't know if you're speaking English or not. But I need you to understand something: a whale is just a whale. I *will* kill Contemptible Blue."

"Hast thou *not* heard the tales, then?" Abbadon asked. "Hast thou not heard that this whale, who is unmistakable by virtue of his impossible size, hath been descried by whaling men as far back as five centuries ago? Contemptible Blue is not of this Earth. Nay, he is an abomination from Hell, and he can not be hunted. He is smarter than any mere man. I must go. If Contemptible Blue kills me before I reach the shore, then please know that I hath made peace with my death. And remember, Captain, the only reason thou art still alive out here at sea is because *he's* allowed it, in some strange, fleeting fit of empathy. Once his mind is changed, the sea shall become thy grave."

Once "The Abbadon Show" was *finally*

over and Abbadon said his final peace, he boarded the small, rickety whaleboat and began to row off towards an uncertain fate. I made sure to get his home address before he left so that I could bill him for the whaleboat. I was sad to see him go—that guy could really shred on the fife. As he sailed away, he called back to me, "Thou looketh sick, Captain. Thou art white as a ghost."

"You should see the *other* guy," I said, even though it didn't make sense.

Right after Abbadon's departure, my fever and nausea seemed to grow more intense. Also, my gums started to feel weird, like they were too big for my mouth. I ran a finger across them to investigate and a bunch of my teeth fell out, just like in that dream that I have every night. I was dizzy and having trouble standing. Finally, I lost all sense of balance and crumbled to the floor of the main deck, bathed in the pale moonlight with the frigid evening air gnawing at my skin. A couple of my crew members ran to my aid, but they didn't really know what to do so they just started swabbing the deck as if that would help.

I began to feel myself slipping out of consciousness. I felt like I was dying, and even though I'd been pronounced dead several times in the past, I was still a little scared. There was only one thing I could do: I ordered one of my crew members to go fetch Dr. Moseley *stat*—I wanted to tell him off before dying.

"And if I *do* die out here, tell my loved ones I killed Contemptible Blue," I muttered to the lingering crew members.

"All right, who are your loved ones?" one of them asked. I couldn't think of any, which reminded me why I decided to go hang out in the middle of the ocean in the first place. I finally passed out, and when I woke up hours later, I woke up on a ship that was no longer mine.

XIV.

The Hold

When I reawoke I was in a cold sweat, feeling like all my insides were tangled up. I was chained to a pipe in a dingy, unlit room somewhere aboard The S.S. Captain Fortnight's Big Boat. *This better not be the BOWELS of the ship*, I thought to myself.

I yanked at the pipe to try and pull loose, but my whole body felt weak, which was weird considering all my big muscles. I cried out for help (in a brave way) and a few moments later I heard the sound of footsteps outside the door. "Who's there!? Free me at once!" I yelled.

"I cannot, Captain Fortnight," I heard a voice say. It was Dr. Moseley, that bloodthirsty cannibal savage with the medical degree. "You're quite sick," he continued. "Have you done anything today that may've put you at risk of contracting illness, Captain?"

"No!"

"And yesterday?"

"I woke up, wrote some shanties, skipped dinner, fell into a crate of dirty harpoons, got pecked by a wild bird a bunch, fell into a big, raw pile of whale shit—same as the day before."

"I see now. All right, you're being quarantined temporarily. I'm going to get you help, mate. We're going to sail back to shore. You need medicine. I have searched the ship and found none. For the time being, it's imperative that we keep you away from the rest of the crew. This shall only take but a few days."

"Taking me back to shore? I HATE it there! I haven't even killed Contemptible Blue, that whale that I hate for no reason!"

"You're obsessed, Captain. You're beginning to sound like the late Captain Ted," Dr. Moseley said.

"Where am I?" I asked.

"In the cargo hold," said the doctor-savage.

"The freaking *bowels* of the ship!?" I asked angrily.

I heard someone else join the doctor outside. "Captain?" the new voice called out. It was Kragg. "How're ye feelin'?" he asked.

"I feel *fine!* On an unrelated note: fetch me my diarrhea bucket. That's an *order.*"

"Captain, ye've fallen ill, and dreadfully so," Kragg insisted. "Did ye not visit a doctor before shippin' out?"

"Kragg," I said, "let me out now or I'm putting a *million* points on your record!"

"Nooo!" Kragg yelled, then started crying. "Oh, my dear captain," he sniffled, "I wish I could do just that. I wish I could let ye out—with my whole heart and soul I do—but I can not. Nay, Captain, not til ye're cured. The good health and well being of yer entire crew is at stake. Oh,

Captain, we've lost too many men already! Milton, Abbadon, and just this morn, our dear fellow seaman Bartleby fell off the mast-head to his death!"

"Well, we'll find another upright bass player," I said.

"Captain, that is another concern: the crew fears ye're more interested in yer little band than being a captain!" Kragg told me.

"Listen Kragg," I said, "I don't trust you to lead this voyage! Who's manning the helm!?"

"I am," Kragg said. "Surely ye remember, Captain, that I've been in charge of navigation since we first left shore. I confess, Captain, that I am fearful, for the storm is soon to hit, but I'll manage."

"Kragg, you have no right to do this— you're terribly unattractive."

"Captain," Dr. Moseley interrupted, "I will be taking over as captain temporarily. I was a captain for years before studying medicine, mate."

"What!? Is this a... mutiny!?"

"This is no mutiny!" Kragg insisted. "My dear captain, our hearts break in two to've done what we've done, but we've done what we must!"

"*Two* million points!" I yelled.

"Noooo!" Kragg yelled.

"Listen Captain," said Dr. Moseley, "I know you're not able to see things clearly right now, but it's quite possible you've developed ocean madness. You show the symptoms. Rage and paranoia, most apparently. It often happens to sailors when they fall ill. We're going to take care of it."

"*Real* mature, guys," I yelled out. I tend to infantilize authority figures like that when they try to exert authority over me. It's just an effective way to bring them down. It's good on bosses and teachers and police officers. *What are we in HIGH school, officer!? Loosen the cuffs, please!*

Anyway...

"Oh, this is *pathetic*," I continued to yell. "Just be *adults* about this—come in here and fight me."

I heard Kragg and Dr. Moseley walk off, leaving me once again all alone in that tiny little cargo hold. "Grow up!" I yelled as they went.

With the backstabbing Dr. Moseley now captaining my ship, I vowed to escape and regain control of what was rightfully mine: Kragg's dead dad's boat.

XV.

Psychological Warfare

"The *bowels* of the ship, of all places," I muttered angrily to myself every time I reawoke there in the cargo hold. "Just unbelievable."

I don't know how much time I spent in there. I fell in and out of consciousness frequently and I was beginning to grow delirious. If only I could free one of my hands, then that might be enough to kill myself. I yanked and yanked at the pipe with what little strength I had left, but it was hopeless. Killing myself was a mere pipe dream.

Then I heard footsteps outside in the hallway. "Who's there?" I cried.

"Aldous," a voice responded. "Do you know where the bathroom is?"

"There isn't one. Hey, you're the one who's afraid of ghosts, right?" I asked.

"Uhh, no," Aldous said sheepishly, doing a bad job of lying.

"Austin," I yelled, "this is your *captain* speaking!"

"I know," said Aldous. "Sorry you got sick."

"That's the *least* of my worries, Arfton. I'm afraid there's bigger fish to fry. Bad news, bud: the ship's haunted."

"Haunted!?" Aldous cried. "Oooh no no no no no! Not again!"

"It's true, Dalton. Don't you hear the whispers at night, when the crew is asleep and all is quiet? Ghostly whispers haunt our vessel. Just *listen.*"

Aldous quieted down for a moment, and from behind the door of the hold, I whispered in a ghostly voice, "*Ooooh, it's me, the ghost of Captain Ted, haunting the ship because I have unfinished business, or whatever.*"

"Oh no no no no no no!" Aldous cried in a panic. "No!"

"Listen Atticus," I said, using my regular voice again, "if we don't exercise the ship immediately, I fear the ghost of Captain Ted will wreak havoc on us, August. We're talkin' about some really spooky shit here."

"Oh my god, please, no!" Aldous shrieked.

"You gotta let me out, Ashton. I can

exercise the ship. I spent a few years in the priesthood."

"I thought you were an atheist."

"I was just kidding," I said. That was really tough for me, because I don't necessarily believe in the afterlife as it's described biblically and I don't care for how religion fails to acknowledge moral gray areas, so...

"But... but your disease," Aldous continued.

"Listen Ogden, you've always been my favorite crew member," I said.

"Really!?" Aldous said excitedly.

"Yeah, sure," I said. "Can you let me out?"

After a few seconds of quiet deliberation, Aldous scampered off and then returned a few minutes later with a mincing knife, a blade used for cutting whale blubber. It took forever for Aldous to saw through my chains with that dull blade, but when he finally did I pushed past him and locked him in the hold behind me, then made a mad dash for the decks where we kept the spare harpoons.

Deathly ill, nearly to the point of madness, I stormed down the quiet halls of my ship, toothless and foaming at the mouth, my body splotched with rashes, muttering to myself about harpooning the new captain. I must have looked awful. I was glad there was no girls on the ship.

XVI.

Lower Yer Harpoon

It was night, and the storm we'd been warned about was finally hitting and ravaging my vessel. Outside, heavy rain pounded the decks and the howl of the ocean wind was deafening. Still hot with a deadly fever, I let the rain cool me off before going to settle the score with Moseley, the total *loser* who used to be a renowned sea captain and then got a license to study medicine.

I heard a voice cry out from behind me. It was Dr. Moseley, draped in a heavy raincoat, wielding a harpoon of his own. "Fortnight! What in the bloody hell are you doing out of the hold!?"

"*You*," I said to the doctor, pointing a harpoon at him, "*you* stole my boat! This whaling adventure was *way* more fun before you came along! Do the right thing here and jump off the boat," I insisted.

The waves were furious and the wind relentless, violently rocking The S.S. Captain Fortnight's Big Boat and making it hard to stand, let alone aim a harpoon at a doctor, which I was normally very good at. "Drop that harpoon, Captain," Dr. Moseley insisted. "You've got ocean madness, mate. Drop it now or I'll strike."

"Put *your* harpoon down! I *can't* go back home," I yelled.

"Put *your* harpoon down," Dr. Moseley yelled back.

"No, put *your* harpoon down," I yelled.

"Lower your harpoon at once!" he yelled.

"Umm, actually, no, *you* lower *your* harpoon!" I yelled.

"Not until *you* lower *your* harpoon!" he yelled.

"Okay well then actually we've got a huge problem here because I'm not gonna lower *my* harpoon until *you* lower *your* harpoon, so I don't know what to tell you, buddy. I mean it is what it is," I said.

"Men, lower yer harpoons, please!" a new voice cried out. It was Kragg. He was right behind me, pointing a harpoon at me.

"Oh, *grow up,*" I said. "Lower your harpoon, you *baby.*"

"Captain, I insist that ye lower *yer* harpoon!" Kragg said.

"Oh my god would you guys *please* lower your harpoons!" a new voice cried out. It was one of my crew members. The whole crew had heard all the yelling and come out to the main deck to investigate, still in their pajamas. I'd have to be sure to have a talk with them about dress code, just as soon as I finished killing Dr. Moseley.

The crew members were clutching harpoons of their own, so I was outnumbered and outharpooned. Finally, I conceded defeat and lowered my harpoon. All the crew members breathed a collective sigh of relief and lowered their harpoons in return. "Wow, that was crazy," one of them said with a chuckle.

"Hey, we're in international waters, right?" I asked.

"Yes," Dr. Moseley said.

"Great," I said, then quickly raised my harpoon again and hurled it at the doctor, only narrowly missing him.

Dr. Moseley fired back and harpooned me straight through the thigh, which was definitely a violation of the Hippocratic Oath. "Savage!" I yelled, before throwing another harpoon and sticking him through the shoulder. Then, the whole crew started to freak out. Egbert *really* panicked and covered his eyes with one hand and just randomly hurled his harpoon. It nicked Kragg's neck. Kragg instinctively hurled his harpoon back in return but missed Egbert and accidentally harpooned Wigmund through the forearm instead. Langdon panicked and ran and jumped off the side of the boat, and when Egbert saw that, he burst into tears and just started hysterically running around in circles. Just straight up running around in circles on the main deck. He tripped and accidentally harpooned Reginald's hand off. Norman threw a harpoon at Egbert, I think because they had some sort of drama going on behind the scenes or something (not really sure what was going on there), and got him right through the ribs. Then Norman was overcome with guilt and yelled,

"Oh my god, I killed Egbert! I can't leave witnesses!" and aimed his harpoon at me, ready to take me out, but I threw one of *my* harpoons first and took one of his ears off. Right at that moment, Aldous, the crew member that I had imprisoned in the cargo hold, ran out onto the main deck. "Hey, Captain Fortnight locked me in the hold!" he yelled, in tears. Then he noticed all the mayhem and panicked and tried to run back to the hold to hide but he tripped over his own feet and knocked himself out cold.

"Oh Lord!" Kragg sobbed, holding the harpoon wound on the side of his neck. "Captain Fortnight, what've ye done!?"

"It's the curse of The Ted," Dr. Moseley muttered. "All men who captain this ship lose it eventually. This is what happens." He pulled the harpoon out of his shoulder and, before passing out, managed to finish by whispering, "*No one survives.*"

Contemptible Blue

"I do," I insisted. "*I* survive."

XVII.

This Ship Was Never Yours

The rain continued to spill and the waves continued to crash upon the deck, combining with the blood of the crew of The S.S. Captain Fortnight's Big Boat and flooding the ship red. "I guess that's why they call it the Red Sea!" I joked, just to lighten the mode. "We're not even on the Red Sea," one of my crew members muttered. I asserted that the joke was still solid.

The crew writhed around on the floor of the main deck, holding their harpoon wounds and whimpering. I saw Kragg pluck the harpoon out of his shoulder and finally stand. "Oh, merciless sea!" he screamed, just being dramatic. "Ye've done it once again, just the same as ye did afore. Ye've driven the brave crew of The Ted to madness! Oh, what sort of wicked curse is this that's befallen The Ted!?"

"It's not called The Ted," I told Kragg.

"Fortnight," he said grimly, "indeed it *is* called The Ted, for it belonged to my father, and still it does. This ship was never yours. Ye're going to kill me. Of that I am certain. And yet, Fortnight, I'll forgive ye. Here, in my final waking moments, I'll forgive ye, for I know it is simply that the curse of The Ted has befallen ye and ye've gone mad. 'Tis just as the doctor said, Fortnight. This is the wicked misfortune that befalls all men who try to hunt Contemptible Blue—who try to do the unfathomable. The universe intervenes, and all goes according to the Lord's plan in the end. The universe intervenes when men so small as ourselves overstep our bounds."

Just then, while Kragg was practicing for his audition for the role of "Overdramatic Baby #1," his attention was seized by something out at sea. His eyes widened and his jaw dropped. I looked back, and that's when, finally, I got my first look at *him*. It was my whale. *My Behemoth, My Bane, My Contemptible Blue.* I *swear* it wasn't a dolphin this time. He looked *just* like the whales I had seen in *Let's Color Whales*, the professional whaling manual that Kragg showed me.

Except there was one difference: he was bigger than I could have ever imagined. He was at least twice as long as the ship, and he was about twice as wide as the ship, and he had two more flippers than the ship had and one more dorsal fin. He was about 200 yards out, slicing through the violent waves and torpedoing *straight* for The S.S. Captain Fortnight's Big Boat on our port side, blowing a big spout of water out of his gross blowhole. "Oh, *get* a life," I yelled to Contemptible Blue upon realizing he was about to destroy my ship.

"Good heavens," Kragg said. "As I live and breathe, Contemptible Blue."

Kragg grabbed his harpoon and hobbled over to the side of the deck, struggling to endure the heavy winds and keep his feet planted on the bloody, wet floor. There was a certain fire in his eyes. He leaned against the bulwark, gripping it desperately for support, cocked back his weapon and hurled it. The vicious winds amplified the harpoon's speed, sending it straight through Contemptible Blue's head, but he didn't flinch. As he continued to speed towards the boat, Kragg gathered up the harpoons of his fellow injured crew members and chucked them at the whale, sticking each one square in his head. Still, Blue was unfazed, and drew nearer and nearer.

With Contemptible Blue only seconds away from tearing through the ship, I calmed myself and quietly accepted my death. I quickly scribbled "No will or testament" across my chest and waited.

Right as he was about to headbutt The S.S. Captain Fortnight's Big Boat to pieces, he was suddenly jerked down beneath the water by his tail. Seconds later, billows of blood and flesh floated up to the surface, turning the black ocean blood red.

"What the hell was that?" I asked Kragg, even though he was stupid.

"He... he was eaten. I guess that *wasn't* Contemptible Blue," Kragg said, his voice quivering from fear. We heard some blood-curdling, beastly wail ring out beneath the surface of the water, and then the ocean seemed to explode as a second whale came torpedoing out of the water and up into the sky, blocking out the moon as he soared directly over our ship. Time seemed to slow down as we watched him hang over us in the sky, his mouth still bloody from his feast.

"*That's* Contemptible Blue," Kragg said.

Just as "Contemptible Blue" was about to dive back into the deep on our starboard size, the head of a third, even larger whale popped out from beneath the waves with its jaws agape, swallowed whale #2 whole and disappeared back into the water.

"All right, *that's* Contemptible Blue," Kragg said.

Kragg and I began to panic, holding each other in our arms and apologizing profusely. "I'm so sorry you got harpooned in the shoulder, man," I told Kragg.

"I'm sorry I brought ye out here, Captain, only to have ye get killed by Contemptible Blue," Kragg said.

"That *was* pretty fucked up," I agreed.

A heavy force struck the ship from below, rocking the vessel and knocking Kragg and I onto the floor of the deck. Then I felt a vague, disorienting sense of movement I couldn't make sense of, until finally I noticed the bow of the ship being pushed slowly into the sky by some driving force beneath us, until the entire ship was perpendicular with the water. Kragg and I clung desperately onto a capstan to keep from sliding down the length of the deck like a vertical waterslide and plunging into the briny deep below us. As we held on, we watched the rest of the crew members, who'd all gone unconscious after suffering their wounds, slide down the deck and disappear into the ocean below. Contemptible Blue continued to drive the bow of The S.S. Captain Fortnight's Big Boat further and further back, until finally the boat tipped backwards, landing upside down in the water. I blacked out just as I felt the force of Contemptible Blue's body crashing down atop the upturned S.S. Captain Fortnight's Big Boat and smashing the entire vessel to pieces.

XVIII.

Dead Man's Float

When I regained consciousness, I was leagues beneath the ocean. I know people use the word "leagues" too lightly, but I really was way down there. I opened my eyes and all I could see was black. I tried to swim to the surface of the water, but I was so disoriented I couldn't even figure out which way was up. *This is how they 'get' you,* I thought to myself for some reason. Finally, I gave up, calmed myself and quietly accepted my death. I relaxed my body, then immediately floated back up to the surface. *Of course,* I thought to myself, *the dead man's float.* Yet another in a long list of situations that I managed to get out of by pretending to be dead.

The storm had finally passed and the ocean was calm. The water around me was still red with blood, and I was surrounded by the debris of my wrecked ship. I spotted a life preserver a couple dozen feet away, swam over to it and grabbed on. *I'm NOT gonna die out here,* I promised myself. Then I spotted a harpoon floating nearby and swam over to grab it so that I could kill myself. Unfortunately, the tip had been broken off and it was too dull. "That's how they 'get' you," I said aloud.

It was the dead of night. I was cold and still sick with my strange cocktail of nautical illnesses. It was safe to say that at this point, this whaling trip did not play out the way I'd hoped. The thing about books like *Moby Dick* and other nautical fiction is they never acknowledge the possibility of the boat getting wrecked. There's never one where the boat gets messed up.

As I continued to tread water out there in the ocean, I grew hungry. It was too bad there's nothing edible in the ocean. Just billions of fish. At least I had plenty of perfectly good saltwater to drink. The salt makes it taste better.

The sun finally began to rise and I could see more clearly. I spotted one of the lifeboats from The S.S. Captain Fortnight's Big Boat, and it appeared to be mostly unharmed, against all odds. I swam over to it and climbed in. The bright morning sun wreaked havoc on my rash. I felt like hell, but even still, I kept my eyes peeled for Contemptible Blue, ready for round two. He was still out there somewhere, and somehow, someway, I was going to get the best of him. *He's not THAT big,* I told myself, even though when I tried to recall his image he was too big to fit in my mental frame.

Suddenly, I was startled by the sound of a voice calling out to me from the distance. It was Kragg. I spotted him about 150 yards away, clinging on to a plank of wood from the wreckage, puffing away at his pipe. I rowed over to him and he crawled into my lifeboat. "All aboard!" I said, trying to lighten the mood.

"Captain Fortnight, ye're alive!" Kragg squealed. "'Tis some sort of miracle!"

It was hard for me to pretend like I hadn't already decided, with 100% certainty, that I was going to eat Kragg, but I managed to put on a poker face. "Ahoy," I said, trying to play it casual.

"Oh, what a dreadful wreck that's been made of us!" Kragg yelled. "Our ship, gone! Our crew, all dead! And Contemptible Blue, still out there!"

"This isn't over yet," I insisted. "Contemptible Blue and I have unfinished business."

"Oh, Captain, ye're simply mad. No man in his right mind—no man whose brain has not been rattled by madness and shipwreck—could yet harbor any hopes of killin' that whale after seein' what was seen last night! Ye're free to pursue him if ye wish, but not with my help, for I am not here at sea for Contemptible Blue. I am here to find my stepbrother, Captain Blagg."

"Look Kragg, I'm gonna eat you," I said, unable to keep up the facade any longer. "I just am, man, straight up. It ain't personal, but a guy's gotta eat. I mean, it is what it is, man. I don't know how else to say it, buddy—I'm gonna eat ya. I'll probably start with your thighs—looks like you got some good meat on those bad boys. Then I'm thinkin' maybe I'll go for the gut next. Go ahead and pop that shirt off and let me see what I'm workin' with there, my man."

"Captain!" Kragg shouted. "Enough! All we have out here is one another!"

"But I'm hungry!"

"I'll catch ye a fish!"

"Yuck!"

"Wait now, Captain—look!" Kragg said, pointing behind me. I turned to look and spotted a big ship way off in the distance. It must have been

500 feet long, with some sort of radar tower built into it that stood so tall you couldn't see where it ended in the sky. The ship was painted camouflage blue and moved fast, leaving a mile-long trail of billowy white water in its wake.

"A destroyer!" Kragg proclaimed. "Perhaps a vessel of the US Navy. She's movin' fast. Captain Fortnight, ye've no hope of makin' way on her if ye row alone. Collect yerself as well ye can, quit yer talk of eatin' me alive, and work alongside me. I'll help ye row."

"Kragg?" I asked.

"Yes, Captain?"

"I sometimes have trouble understanding what you're saying."

"My apologies."

"It's okay to use smaller words."

"I understand."

"I just feel like it takes you a really long time to say things."

"Yes, yes, of course."

"It's just really exhausting."

"All right."

"It just sucks, man, you know?"

"Yes, I understand."

"So, what were you saying about that ship?"

"I was saying, Captain, that if ye don't eat me alive, then I can help ye row yer boat, we can make way on that yonder destroyer ship, and perhaps they'd come to our rescue."

"Okay, see, that's much easier for me to digest. Thank you."

"All right. I'll try to keep my sentences pithy."

"What?"

"I'll try to keep my sentences short."

"Okay, cool. Well, let's go catch that huge boat."

XIX.

The Confederacy For The War On Whalers

As Kragg and I paddled nearer to the massive, mysterious ship, I noticed some words painted on the side of it: "Confederacy for the War on Whalers." I wondered whose ship it was. "Captain," Kragg said to me, "that vessel belongs to The Confederacy for the War on Whalers."

"No *shit*, Kragg."

"Captain, I've heard many a tale of these men. They are vigilantes of the high seas—lubbers of the whale. The Confederacy for the War on Whalers blows up whaleships on sight, for they wish to liberate the whale, despite all her practical utilities. If we are rescued by these men, they must not know us as whalers, but as simple sailors."

A man having a smoke out on the deck of the destroyer finally spotted us rowing after the ship. He ran off and then returned moments later with another man who must have been the captain. He wore an eyepatch and a strange blood-spattered bearskin pea-jacket. There was a gold coat-of-arms pinned proudly on his jacket that read: "Captain Meierhorn, C.W.W." He had a parrot perched on his shoulder, which I thought was trying too hard, but I bit my tongue.

"Ye down there," he called out to us, "I am Captain Meierhorn, benevolent captain of The Confederacy for the War on Whalers! Be ye whalers?"

"Nay," Kragg shouted back. "We are simple sailors. We are not whalers—not nearly so—for we are wise enough to know, Captain, that here in the kingdom of the sea, it is whales who rule!"

"And whalers drool," I added.

"Grand!" yelled Captain Meierhorn. "'Cause *if* ye were whalers, I'd shoot a hole through thy bloody boat and watch ye sink!"

"Ha ha ha, right on, man. That would be the

appropriate manner in which to treat a whaler for sure," I yelled. I was doing a good job at pretending I wasn't a whaler. "Psst, Kragg, I'm doing a good job of pretending I'm not a whaler," I whispered at Kragg.

Captain Meierhorn tossed down a rope ladder and Kragg and I climbed aboard. "Welcome aboard, ye bloody waterlogged bastards!" Captain Meierhorn greeted us.

"Look," I told Captain Meierhorn, "I don't want there to be any secrets between us, so I'm gonna be upfront here: I might have ocean madness."

"Oh, bloody hell!" Captain Meierhorn yelled. "Let's get ye fixed up!"

Captain Meierhorn escorted Kragg and I below the decks and to the stateroom of one of his crew members who had some basic medical training. He gave us each some warm, dry clothes, then stitched up our harpoon wounds and gave me some medicine for my illness. Then, we were escorted to a spare cabin and left to sleep. By morning, I felt as good as new.

After hearing about the slaughter that had occurred on The S.S. Captain Fortnight's Big Boat, the doctor suggested I talk to someone. "You had ought to sail ashore and see a therapist. You must be in tremendous psychological turmoil," he said.

"I'm good, thanks!"

XX.

Don't Trust The Captain

After getting fixed up and sleeping off our trauma, Kragg and I were invited to dine with the rest of The Confederacy for the War on Whalers crew in Captain Meierhorn's stateroom. I was ravenously hungry. I truly could have eaten anything at that point. "We're havin' fish," Captain

Meierhorn announced. I stuck my tongue out and made a gagging sound and pushed my plate away, politely declining. *Welp, I'm gonna eat this guy's bird,* I quietly decided to myself, then asked Captain Meierhorn if his parrot could show me to the bathroom.

As soon as I left Captain Meirhorn's stateroom and was alone with the parrot, my mouth watering, it squawked at me, "Mutiny! Mutiny!"

"What did you say?" I asked the parrot.

"Squawk! Don't trust the captain. SQUAWK!"

"Don't trust the captain? Why not?"

"Squawk! I've said too much! Squawk! He'll kill me! Squawk! This never happened! Squawk! Ocean madness!"

A vague sense of dread came over me. As a general rule I try not to trust birds because they've lied to me in the past but I couldn't help but wonder if this one was telling the truth. I returned to dinner hesitantly, where Captain Meierhorn was in the middle of telling Kragg a little bit about the Confederacy's recent adventures. "Fortnight," Captain Meierhorn greeted me upon my re-arrival, "did ye find a place to go to the bathroom?"

"Uh, yeah," I said.

"Nothing happened!" squawked the parrot. "We talked about the weather! Squawk!"

"All right," said Captain Meierhorn. "I was just regailin' Kragg here with some tales of my many adventures at sea. He's havin' a great time, the maniac. Aren't ye Kragg?"

"Aye," Kragg responded weakly, giving me a grim look. He seemed uncomfortable. "Captain Meierhorn," he continued, "why don't ye tell Captain Fortnight here what ye told me in his absence?"

"Well," said Meierhorn, "The Confederacy for the War on Whalers hath been doing God's work for nigh on three decades. I've been the captain since the Confederacy's inception. Men, tell Captain Fortnight how many whaling ships hath been blown to hell by the Confederacy for the War on Whalers!"

"Three-hundred and fifty-four," the captain's dead-eyed crew replied in unison.

"Aye!" yelled Captain Meierhorn loudly, pounding the dinner table with his fist. "Now, my lads, tell Captain Fortnight how many whales, even by conservative estimates, that we warriors of God must've saved in all our years asea!"

"Thousands and thousands," the crew responded weakly, sounding like they were reading off a script.

"Anything else ye wish to say, men?" Meierhorn asked the crew.

"You're nice," the crew responded again in their lifeless monotone.

"Ha ha ha, that is correct!" Captain

Meierhorn bellowed. Then he got all riled up and smashed his brandy snifter on the floor, then turned to me and Kragg and said, "Ye two men are lucky to've found thyselves in my company, ye bastards! Look at ye, dining alongside such an esteemed crew, under the command of such a decorated captain!"

"Ocean madness!" squawked the parrot.

"Excuse me for a moment," Captain Meierhorn said. He took the parrot and left the stateroom, then we heard a gunshot from outside. He returned a few moments later covered in parrot feathers. "My bird got away," he said. "Anyway, laddies," he continued, turning to me and Kragg, "we're happy to have ye aboard, but we'll have to put ye to work, of course. There are no free rides on the Confederacy."

"What manner of work?" asked Kragg.

"Deck swabbing."

"Fuck!" I yelled, before storming out and

going outside to cool down. I was pissed off at Captain Meierhorn for screwing me over like that, and it kind of made me wish that I had gone ahead and eaten his bird earlier, but it was too late now because it had flown away, apparently.

XXI.

Whaleship USS Maine

The next day Kragg and I were put to work. Captain Meierhorn supplied us with mops and instructed us to get to swabbing. "Ye're doing God's work out here, lads," he assured us. "We all are."

Kragg started swabbing the deck as ordered. I only *pretended* to swab it: I moved my mop back and forth, but I was holding it inches above the deck so that I wasn't technically swabbing. It took the same amount of effort as actually swabbing, but I felt like I was getting away with something. "Psst," I whispered to Kragg, "I'm not even swabbing the deck, dude."

"Captain Fortnight," he whispered back, "let us not be swept up into the violent affairs of the Confederacy, for I do not trust Captain Meierhorn. There is a look in his eye, or rather a certain strange absence in them, that I saw in yer eyes, too, when ye nearly succumbed to ocean madness. Let us draw no attention to ourselves, but rather do our work quietly and with no air of begrudgement, until finally the Confederacy stops ashore on some port of call, and then let us flee."

I agreed with Kragg but I didn't like that he was bossing me around so I slapped his mop out of his hand and threw it into the ocean. "Come on, man," he said.

Just then, one of Captain Meierhorn's parrots, of which there were many perched throughout the Confederacy ship, started squawking, "Whalers! Whalers!" It had spotted a whaleship out in the distance, sailing abreast the Confederacy ship. The parrot flew off to alert the captain, and Meierhorn appeared on the deck moments later with the rest of his crew following behind him. They looked pale and uneasy, like they were dreading something to come.

"Aye, 'tis a whaleship indeed!" Captain Meierhorn said, watching the ship pass through his telescope. "Let us send these bumbling whalers the way of Davy Jones!"

"Who's that?" I asked.

Captain Meierhorn shrugged me off and pulled a stick of dynamite out of the inside pocket of his bearskin pea-jacket. "My harpoon!" he commanded. One of his crew members, looking white as a ghost and full of dread, fetched him a harpoon. Captain Meierhorn carefully tied his stick of dynamite to the harpoon, kissed the tip, lit the fuse, cocked it back and hurled it with seemingly superhuman strength. It pierced through the air and stuck right through the side of the whaleship. Just then, as I squinted my eyes to get a closer look at the ship, I noticed something written on the side of it: "USS Maine." It seemed like a weird name for a whaling vessel.

"Captain," Kragg said to Captain Meierhorn, "I believe that's a United States naval shi—"

The dynamite blew and I covered my ears as I watched the USS Maine explode into a million pieces, leaving a smoldering pile of wood behind in the ocean.

"Victory!" Captain Meierhorn cried, jumping up and down and waving his arms in the air. "Another whaleship down! Aye! Another dozen whalers blown to smithereens! Vic-tor-y! Vic-tor-y! Come on, men!"

The rest of the crew reluctantly joined in on the captain's celebration, waving their hands in the air limply and jumping up and down and murmuring, "Vic-tor-y, vic-tor-y, vic-tor-y." They sounded dead inside. Kragg and I looked at each other, sharing a similar expression of dread. "We must abandon ship and run from this man, *now*," he whispered to me. "We must find a way back to shore."

"But what about Contemptible Blue?" I whispered back.

"Captain, have ye lost yer way? I've told ye once already that I shipped out *not* for Contemptible Blue, but for Captain Blagg. Yer vendetta with this whale is of no great concern to me. And furthermore, if ye so much as cast a sideways glance at a whale while aboard this destroyer, Captain Meierhorn will put a harpoon through yer head."

"Better men have tried," I told Kragg.

Captain Meierhorn's crew continued their celebration, under strict orders from their captain. "Keep celebrating!" Captain Meierhorn insisted.

"Louder! Happier! Be *happier!*"

"Vic-tor-y, vic-tor-y," they carried on murmuring. A few of them started crying mid-celebration, still continuing to cheer. It was truly one of the most unsettling things I had ever seen in my life, and I had just seen a United States naval ship get bombed. Plus I'd been hanging out with a guy with no face.

Captain Meierhorn insisted that we all get drunk to further celebrate the successful sinking of that "whaleship." That was a relief, because I really needed something to take the edge off—I was pretty shaken up after witnessing the USS Maine explode. Plus, I was starting to suspect that Captain Meierhorn had killed that bird.

XXII.

GOD'S WORK

That evening, the brandy was flowing as we celebrated the sinking of the USS Maine. I was a little uncomfortable with the circumstances of the celebration, but that didn't stop me from getting drunk. Few things ever do.

The crew of the Confederacy drank hard. The captain drank to celebrate, while the crew drank to forget about the fact that their captain was freely blowing up non-whaleships. Captain Meierhorn couldn't have been a very intuitive guy, because he seemed to think everybody was having a great time. "What a grand party!" he kept yelling, while his men drank silently and stared at the floor.

During the party, Kragg pulled me aside to speak in private. "Captain Fortnight, may we discuss our escape?" he asked. "The captain and his crew are preoccupied."

"Let's worry about it after the party," I suggested. "Let's just drink up and have a good time. We've had a tough couple of days: our ship sank, Contemptible Blue got away, Your Worst Night-Maritime broke up..."

"We're not safe on these decks, Captain Fortnight. I feel dark clouds a-lingerin' over this ship. Captain, have ye not stared into the deadened eyes of Captain Meierhorn's crewmen? They are cowering, and it appears they fear for their lives, as well I believe they should."

"Kragg, do you like me?" I asked—I was pretty drunk. I get a little "mushy" on brandy.

"Aye, Captain, but please, let me show ye something I've found."

"You're so cool, Kragg. You're like, the nicest guy," I slurred. My inhibitions were pretty low.

"Look here, Captain," Kragg insisted. He pulled a small journal out of the pocket of his monkey jacket and showed it to me. "While Captain Meierhorn and his slavish soldiers were distracted with their celebration, I crept away for but a moment, and sneaked into the captain's stateroom. I found this. 'Tis the captain's log. *Look*."

Kragg opened the log and showed me a passage, which read:

"I am the o n e t r u e CAPTAIN and I am doing G O D ' S W O R K. Kill kill kill kill kill all whalers. Sink every ship and ask questions LATER if EVER. I WILL NOT BE DISOBEYED AND I WILL TAKE ORDERS FROM N O M A N."

"Wow, Captain Meierhorn's actually a pretty good writer," I admitted.

"He's gone mad," Kragg said direly.

"Hey Kragg, if we're both still single in six months, do you—" I began to ask. Oh boy, I was way too drunk. Luckily Kragg cut me off. "We're in grave danger," he warned.

"Okay look, let me just get another drink and we'll figure it out," I slurred. I went and rejoined the rest of the crew as the brandy continued to flow. The captain was still barking at his men to celebrate harder. "We've earned this!" he kept shouting.

"Yeah... yeah," the crew would say back unenthusiastically while staring at the floor.

I blacked out shortly after Kragg showed me the captain's log. I woke up in my cabin the next morning with a nasty brandy hangover and a half finished container of Chinese food on my chest. I'm not sure where I got it. Having slept off my drunkenness, the gravity of what Kragg had showed me last night was beginning to sink in and I felt an urgent need to get off that ship. Even worse than that: I was pretty humiliated thinking back to all those things I'd said to Kragg last night. Also, I remembered that I sent a pretty regretful message-in-a-bottle to an ex of mine.

I heard a furious knocking at my door. It was Captain Meierhorn. "Time for work, lad! Wake up, wipe the mornin' from thine eyes and get to swabbin' the deck!" he demanded.

Kragg was already awake and hard at work. I joined him begrudgingly and explained to him that I was really drunk last night and I didn't mean all those nice things I said. He was bummed.

I was way off course. *Look how far I've fallen,* I thought to myself. Once a great(ish) sea captain, here I was *now,* just a lowly swabbie taking orders from an insane pro-whale vigilante. I began to think that I might never kill my whale. Best case scenario at this point was I make it back to land and maybe suicide bomb a fish hatchery or something.

As we were hard at work swabbing the deck, another crew member came over and joined us. He didn't acknowledge us, but instead stared straight at the ocean as he spoke, so as not to draw attention. "Psst," he whispered. "Mutiny?"

"What?" I whispered back.

"A mutiny," he repeated. "Against the captain. Art thou with us?"

"I art," I said. "Kragg? You art?"

"Aye," Kragg agreed.

"We must be quiet. Captain Meierhorn hath eyes and ears all about the ship, and privacy is elusive," the crew member said, gesturing subtly towards a parrot perched upon the bulwark. "My name is Hogg," the crew member said.

"Sorry to hear that," I said.

"I hath been a soldier of the Confederacy since its inception, long, long ago," Hogg continued, still speaking in a hushed whisper. "In our infancy, Captain Meierhorn led this crusade with valor and intentions pure. We sunk only whaleships, and smiled and waved brightly at other, non-whaling vessels as they passed. I hath since seen my captain fall to ocean madness. I hath seen the man—his soul long-lost and left behind in the offing—execute every man who hath accused him of sickness. It is his claim that God speaks to him, but no god of mine would give such harrowing commandments—commandments to bomb each and every passing craft on sight and ask questions later, if ever at all. The time hath come to intervene and let the Confederacy fall, for so many innocent men hath died, and art we not all good Christians here?"

"Yes," Kragg said.

"Well actually—" I began to clarify.

"The crew hath conferred about a mutiny in the quieter and more private hours," Hogg continued, "but nary a single man in our company hath captain's experience. Had we overthrown our crooked captain long ago, we'd hath stranded ourselves asea. But oh, what sweet fortune hath befallen us, for we hath among us now a captain."

Then Hogg nodded toward me, continuing by saying, "Certainly, with thine experience as a captain, thou art equipped to sail us back ashore to the safe haven of the coast, aye Captain?"

"Me?" I asked.

"Yes. Thou *art* a captain, art thou not, Captain Fortnight?" Hogg asked.

"Of course I art," I insisted. "You know what, though? Kragg needs the practice because he's such a bad captain, so you should let *him* give it a whirl."

"I am green, Hogg," Kragg admitted, "but I could manage. If we kill yer cruel dictator, I could sail us ashore safely, and would gladly do so, for I too, in weeks gone by, have seen carnage and little of anything else, and I long to once again return to land."

"All right," whispered Hogg. "I hath been planning this mutiny for nigh on four years."

"Ah yes, about 104 fortnights," I

interjected.

"Yes," Hogg said, pretending not to be impressed. "Meierhorn keeps a vigilant eye out," he continued, "and that cruel, pugilistic barbarian of a man is always prepared for a fight, for he hath long anticipated some manner of revolt against him. We hath no hope of ambushing the sober captain—not with his many wary parrots surveying our every move. But when the captain drinks, he doth so in gluttonous excess, drinking himself careless. When next we sink a whaleship, the captain will celebrate as he always does, and when finally he hath drunk himself drunk enough to let down his guard—when he hath drunk himself so drunk that not even a warning from his loyal parrots could ready him for a bloody confrontation—we shall strike."

"What?" I asked.

"I understand, Hogg," whispered Kragg.

"Back to work!" squawked one of the

nearby parrots. "Work will set you free! Squawk!"

XXIII.

Get A Load Of THIS Motherfucker, Right!?

Weeks passed aboard the Confederacy with no action. The ocean seemed to be dead—we didn't cross paths with any other ships, luckily for them, and so things moved slow on the mutiny front. Kragg and I continued to quietly go about our swabbing duties. I grew more and more miserable every day. This whole nautical adventure was essentially supposed to be a vacation, and somehow I ended up with a full-time job. It was like if you took a vacation to Thailand, but then, you end up *managing* a brothel. It really was just like my vacation to Thailand.

Captain Meierhorn's insanity was the perpetual elephant in the room. We all knew he was mad, but no one dared speak about it aloud—

not with his guard parrots listening in on our every word and watching our every move. The crew communicated only in subtle, grim glances. Captain Meierhorn would pace around the ship, muttering things to himself like, "Kill kill kill," and, "They'll all die in a watery grave," and, "Sink the entire planet," and all of us on the crew would give each other these little looks that kind of said, *Get a load of THIS motherfucker, right!?*

Finally, one scorching hot morning on the high seas, I spotted a ship cruising peacefully off in the distance while I was pretending to swab the deck. It appeared to be a commercial liner. I squinted my eyes and saw something written on the side of it: "Singles at Sea." *Oh boy, it's a singles cruise,* I thought to myself.

"Look," I said to Kragg, pointing to the cruise liner. Kragg smiled and immediately ran off to inform Captain Meierhorn. Soon, it would be bombs away and the mutiny would finally happen.

Hopefully everyone on that singles cruise had already met someone. It would be nice if they didn't have to go through that alone.

Rather than bomb the ship on sight like he had done with the USS Maine a few weeks earlier, Captain Meierhorn hailed for the cruise ship to come closer. He hopped up and down screaming, "Over here!" They finally spotted us and the two ships drew nearer until we were bow-to-bow with about 20 feet of distance in between us. The captain of the doomed cruise liner ascended from the bridge to the foredeck, wearing an open bathrobe, puffing leisurely on a pipe and drinking out of a coconut. "Ahoy!" he said. "I'm Captain Donovan! How's the sea treatin' ya this mornin', boys?"

"Splendidly!" Captain Meierhorn shouted back. "And how's the whalin', whaler?" he asked with a sinister smile. "How many barrels this season?"

"Oh, we're not whalers," Captain Donovan clarified. "Just a boatful of lonely lovers makin' our way 'round the world, baby!"

"Have ye any news from the coast, *whaler*?" asked Captain Meierhorn.

"Sure! We just stopped ashore on a brief excursion a few days ago. I brought a newspaper along. It's all yours, babe!"

Captain Donovan fetched the newspaper out of his robe and tossed it to Captain Meierhorn. "Obliged, *whaler*," said Captain Meierhorn.

"We're not whalers," Captain Donovan said again. "Just a couple hundred singles makin' our way—"

"I've got some news for ye as well!" Captain Meierhorn interrupted. "Today's top headline: Whaleship Singles at Sea Blows Up and Goes to Hell! Here, catch!"

Captain Meierhorn retrieved a stick of his trusty dynamite from his inside jacket pocket, lit it, kissed it and gently tossed it forward to Captain Donovan. Captain Donovan caught it, gave Captain Meierhorn a quizzical look and said, "This would appear to be a lit stick of dynami—"

We all hit the deck and covered our ears as the dynamite blew, blowing the bow off the Singles at Sea and sending it sinking into the ocean. The waves rocked the Confederacy ship and smoke filled the air. When the smoke finally cleared, Captain Meierhorn got up and threw his captain's cap into the air in celebration, hooting and hollering and running a victory lap around the deck of the ship. "So long, wicked whalers, ye bastard sons of whores!" he yelled.

Just as expected, a drunken celebration was to follow. "Bring up the barrels of brandy from the hold!" the captain commanded. "Drink up, men! Long live the Confederacy!"

For once, the crew of The Confederacy for the War on Whalers didn't have to fake their excitement. With the mutiny of Captain Meierhorn on the horizon, there was plenty to celebrate in earnest. The crew dragged up the barrels of brandy stashed away in the cargo hold and we got the party started. I hit the brandy pretty hard. I was really shaken up after seeing that singles cruise explode. I know it *sounds* funny on paper, but in real life it's kind of scary.

We all got good and drunk. Unfortunately, since we were so excited about the impending mutiny, we drank a little *too* much to celebrate and we all passed out way before Captain Meierhorn did. We were all out like lights by around 11 P.M. Captain Meierhorn stayed up all night and partied alone with his birds.

XXIV.

The Confederacy Falls

The next morning I woke up slumped over the bulwark, hungover and tanned to a crisp from the hot summer sun, with a half eaten chicken finger sub on my chest. The rest of the crew were lying on the floor, still fast asleep after a hard night of celebrating a mutiny that didn't happen. My body felt awful from the hangover. Plus, I remembered some things I'd said to Kragg in my drunken state the night before and I was mortified thinking back on them. I think I called him a "hero." *Ugh.*

Captain Meierhorn was still going strong when I woke up. He hadn't stopped drinking yet, and he was still rambling to his parrots about blowing up the Singles at Sea. "It was magnificent, aye!?" he slurred to the parrots as he paced back and forth.

"Yes, Captain, very cool," they said back patronizingly.

I stumbled back onto the deck and that's when something caught my eye. That newspaper we had received from Captain Donovan was lying on the floor, turned to a page with a headline that read: "Your Worst Night-Maritime Rocks Old Barnacle Tavern." I read through the article furiously. It was a glowing review of a concert that had been held back on shore by a band called Your Worst Night-Maritime, fronted by a sea shanty singer named Abbadon. The article mentioned one song in particular called "Throw Away The Stowaway" that had really rocked the Old Barnacle Tavern, apparently.

Abbadon, my old crew member who had abandoned The S.S. Captain Fortnight's Big Boat voyage only weeks ago, had apparently made it back to shore safely and settled into a new career playing sea shanties, including *my* hit single

"Throw Away the Stowaway," using *my* band name, without *my* permission or the permission of his old bandmates (R.I.P.).

I had a new priority, and my revised hit list, in order of importance, went like this: 1. Abbadon 2. Captain Meierhorn 3. Contemptible Blue or an entire fish hatchery.

Captain Meierhorn noticed that I was awake and called out to me. "Good morning, Fortnight," he yelled. "Hell of a party last night, aye lad?"

"Captain Meierhorn, I need to go back to shore, *now*."

"Why?"

"I need to go beat up my old bandmate. It's a whole big thing."

"We've more work to do out here."

Just then, I saw Captain Meierhorn's eyes widen as a look of astonishment washed over his face. I knew that look. He was staring out into the open water behind me. I turned to look for myself, and that's when I saw that, finally, *he'd* returned to me. *My Behemoth, My Bane, My Contemptible Blue.*

Contemptible Blue, that slippery, gargantuan monster that destroyed my ship and broke up my band, was floating peacefully at the surface of the water, letting the waves crash gently down upon his hump. He spouted, firing a jet of billowy white water out of his blowhole and high into the air. Probably some sort of threat. "Hey, fuck you too," I called out to him.

I had forgotten how big he was. He could have flattened a ship *twice* as big as The S.S. Captain Fortnight's Big Boat if he wanted to. The disgusting creature was like the size of a small country. A really *bad* country. (You probably know which one I'm talking about.)

I stood there frozen, marveling at his impossible mass, and in that moment I was sure that he had to be the largest living creature on Earth, which is why I was so terrified when he was suddenly jerked underwater by some unseen second creature—one that had to have been even larger. Billows of bloody bubbles floated to the surface and turned the ocean a familiar shade of red. I was so hopped up on adrenaline that I could hardly make my funny "now I know why they call it the Red Sea" joke but did.

Finally, the *real* Contemptible Blue showed himself. He emerged from the surface of the water, three times as large as the whale he'd just eaten for lunch. He was like the size of a medium-sized country out there—a really, *really* bad one (Austria, probably). He began swimming laps out there in the distance, leaving a trail of blood behind him as he continued to chew up that first whale. Then, he seemed to notice the Confederacy ship and he slowly drew nearer to us. I was expecting him to attack, but instead, he began swimming laps peacefully around the ship.

His guard was down and I could have harpooned him right then and there if only Captain Meierhorn was absent. He squealed like a child at the sight of Contemptible Blue, clapping his hands and whispering, "Come here, my baby."

All the commotion woke up Kragg, and when he wiped his eyes and saw Contemptible Blue circling the destroyer, he nearly keeled over. "Shh," Captain Meierhorn insisted.

Contemptible Blue came to a stop on our starboard side and poked his head out of the water. He seemed to be staring directly at me with his eyes the size of small, desolate planets. Captain Meierhorn waved at him and said, "Hey boy, it's Captain Meierhorn." He spouted at us, showering us with cold, bloody ocean water. Captain Meierhorn laughed. "That's how he says hello," he told Kragg and I. "I recognize this beauty. He's an old friend of the Confederacy. We're one of the few ships he won't sink on sight, for he knows us as an ally. What a gorgeous creature," he said. It creeped me out. I'm just gonna say it: I think Captain Meierhorn jerked off to whales.

There comes a few times in life when you just have to bomb first and worry about the backlash later. Maybe I learned that from Captain Meierhorn. All I knew for *sure* in that moment was I had unfinished business to finally finish, and I wasn't going to let one man with a coat full of dynamite stop me. "Can I borrow your jacket?" I asked Captain Meierhorn. "It's chilly."

"Sure, lad," he said, passing me his jacket.

Contemptible Blue was putting on a show now. He was circling the ship again, twirling in the water as he swam and spouting every which way. Finally, he rocketed himself out of the water, soaring over the Confederacy ship from port to starboard and blocking out the sun, turning the bright sky dim. Captain Meierhorn and Kragg clapped and cheered, but I wasn't impressed. *I jump over shit all the time,* I thought to myself. I lit the fuses on four dynamite sticks and prepared to finally end my hunt.

Contemptible Blue plunged back into the blood-red deep for a moment, then came torpedoing out once more and soaring over our ship again. Just as he was about to reach the peak of his arc over the ship, I swung the dynamite sticks down and back between my legs and hurled them up at him. He swiftly swatted them away with his flipper, sending them right back down from whence they came, which is an expression that I'm using correctly. I watched them fall, still lit, onto the floor of the main deck, then I made a mad dash towards the side and dove overboard. Kragg tried to follow my lead but tripped over one of the passed out crewmen on the way.

As I dropped from the ship to the water, I saw Captain Meierhorn's parrots fly off into the sunset. "We're free!" one of them squawked. "Let's go to the Galapagos!" another squawked.

I plunged into the cold, bloody ocean below, then I heard the excruciating BANG as The Confederacy for the War on Whalers exploded into a ball of fire above me. I knew there'd be no survivors. *At least the crew died peacefully in their sleep, in an explosion,* I told myself.

Except for Kragg. He died conscious and flat on his face. I knew that poor Kragg didn't deserve to go out like that. Plus, I'm pretty sure he died a virgin. As I sank further down into the ocean, I couldn't stop dwelling on the last thing I'd said to him the night before—the last, awful thing I said to him before his death: "You're like a hero to me, Kragg." I would take it back if I could.

Contemptible Blue

XXV.

You Seriously Fucked Dale? Are You Fucking Shitting Me?

I tread water out there in the middle of the ocean for hours, surrounded by the debris of the Confederacy destroyer. The explosion seemed to have scared Contemptible Blue off. Just as I'd always suspected—he was a coward. I sifted through the floating debris trying to find something useful. I came upon the charred badge of Captain Meierhorn, still in pretty good shape. I stuffed it in my jacket pocket to pawn later. "Cha-ching!" I said aloud.

Then, a massive storm hit with no warning. The sky opened up and rain began to pound my head, while thunder cracked in the sky and lightning struck the metal debris around me. The ocean grew unruly. I tried to stay above water as the waves thrashed me, but after a few minutes I grew too tired. I saw a massive tidal wave making its way towards me in the distance, growing larger and larger by the second. I plugged my nose and closed my eyes as it finally hit, plunging me leagues beneath the ocean. I'd *almost* go so far as to say *fathoms* beneath the ocean, but I don't know if that's deeper than leagues.

There I was, back in the briny deep again. All I could think to myself down there was, *Wow, there really is a ton of brine down here.*

They say drowning is the worst way to die, I think because you get all wet. It did indeed seem like a bad way to go out, but nevertheless, I calmed myself and quietly accepted my death. Finally, after a few minutes of being thrashed around underwater, I lost consciousness.

I opened my eyes later to realize I was suddenly at the surface, doing a dead man's float under a clear, orange sky. The storm had passed and the wreckage was gone. I heard a beautiful melody dancing in the air behind me. Someone was singing. I turned around and swam towards it, following the song to its source. I came upon a large rock sticking out of the water and there I found my singer. She was perched upon the rock, wearing a billowy white dress, cooing her sweet song. I knew I was hallucinating, but I didn't care. Why not one final, brief moment of beauty before my death at sea?

The siren woman extended her hand and helped me up. She finished her song, then asked me about myself. I told her my story and she was captivated. She invited me back to the Isle of Sirens, where she and her fellow songstresses of the sea lived. We swam there together and sprawled out in the sand under the warm, romantic light of the moon. Then, ever so softly, our lips touched in a kiss and soon we made love. We fell asleep in each other's arms, naked as the day we were born, out there on the beach.

We went out on a few more dates after that, then after a few months we made it "official." We got married a few years later. After about ten years of that we started to get bored of each other. The separate beds came about 12 years in. At that point, we kind of felt more like roommates than lovers. One day, we got into a pretty big fight because I stayed out too late.

"I was out whaling!" I said.

"Why didn't you just call, then?" the sea siren asked.

"I'm not in the mood tonight, alright?" I said.

"Do you even want to be together anymore?" the sea siren asked.

"Well it's kind of hard when you're always SINGIN' ALL THE GOD DAMN TIME!" I said.

"I *love* to sing, you *know* that about me," the sea siren said.

"Yeah, well, I love to go whaling, so why can't we just each do our *own* thing?" I asked.

"Fine, why don't we just *split up* then? Is that what you want?" the sea siren asked.

"*Fine!*" I said.

"*Fine!*" the sea siren said.

"*Fine!*" I said.

"Captain Fortnight?" the sea siren asked.

"What?" I asked.

"I cheated on you," the sea siren said.

"What? Are you serious? With who?" I asked.

"Dale," the sea siren said.

"Dale!? The guy from work?" I asked.

"Yes," the sea siren said.

"You seriously fucked Dale? Are you fucking shitting me?" I asked.

"No, I'm not," the sea siren said.

"Great. Just *great!* How could you do this!?" I asked.

"Because you haven't made any effort in *twelve* years! You look at me like I'm a *monster.* I'm your *wife!*" the sea siren said.

"What are you even *talking* about?" I asked.

"Look, I think I should go stay at my mother's for a while," the sea siren said.

"Yeah, I think you *should!*" I said.

"Fine. Have a nice life," the sea siren said.

"Fine, *I will,*" I said.

"And I'm taking Captain Fortnight Jr.," she said.

"Fine!"

After she left I went to a singles bar there on the Isle of Sirens and tried to hook up but was unsuccessful because I had let myself go and was pretty fat now. It was a really bad hallucination. I couldn't wait to hurry up and die already.

Contemptible Blue

XXVI.

Was He As Beautiful As They Say?

I finally snapped out of my nightmare hallucination when a sharp pain stung my leg. I was pulled up to the surface of the water and reeled into a sailboat. I collapsed onto the deck, spat up ocean water, tussled the seaweed out of my hair and pulled the hook from my leg. I must have been seconds away from drowning before I was reeled up. I gasped for air for a few minutes before I finally regained my composure.

The storm had passed and the sea was calm now. Some daring fisherman had snagged my leg with his hook. "Hey asshole, I was trying to die down there!" I said.

"You're not a fish," he said to me, looking disappointed.

"Please, do you have anything to eat on this boat?" I asked.

"No, I don't—you're not a fish," he said.

The fisherman, all alone out there on the water in his rickety little sailboat, took me into the cabin, gave me some fresh, warm clothes, and then retreated back outside to get back to fishing while I recovered in the cabin. He returned an hour later, holding two big fish in his hands. "Dinner is served," he said.

"I don't like fish," I told him.

"I don't like people," he said, "but here I am treating you to a free meal, so dine with me and be grateful."

The fisherman was a rail thin, thickly bearded man who'd been out to sea for so long he was growing mold on his skin. He wore a tattered pair of overalls over a shirt that was once white but was now stained yellow from sweat. He stunk of the sea and had a look of sadness and fatigue in his eyes. I asked how we were going to cook the fish.

Contemptible Blue

"I don't bother cooking," he answered, before taking a big bite out of the raw fish. It was so gross that I thought I was gonna puke. I *seriously* almost spewed all over the boat. I was *so* close to hurling, I swear, but I managed to choke it down. I seriously did almost yack though. I was about to freaking ralph everywhere.

"What's your name?" the fisherman asked.

"Captain *Stupid* Idiot Who Fucked Up and Blew Up His Friend," I said, because I was still pretty mad at myself.

"A captain? Of what?" he asked, his mouth full of raw fish.

"I used to whale," I said.

"Were you any good?" he asked.

"No."

"Have you ever heard of Contemptible Blue?"

"Yes. I don't want to talk about it."

"Really? Tell me, Captain: was he as

beautiful as they say?"

"No, he's *ugly*," I said.

"How'd you meet the almighty Contemptible Blue?" he asked.

"I set out to hunt him a few weeks ago. Things have slowed down a little on that front—I'm kind of figuring things out right now—but I'm definitely gonna get back into it soon. I'm just taking a little time for *me* right now. *Definitely* gonna get back into it, though."

"Right," the fisherman said skeptically. "My name is Sebastian. Tell me, Captain Stupid Idiot Who Fucked Up and Blew Up His Friend, with all your knowledge and experience as a whaler, could you *lead* me to Contemptible Blue?"

"If you're thinking of killing Contemptible Blue, then *back off.* He's *mine...* I'm *definitely* gonna get back into it soon."

"*Kill* him!?" Sebastian scoffed. "Oh, Captain, no. Oh heavens, no. I couldn't kill him if I wanted to. He *cannot* be killed. I want *him* to kill *me*."

"What?" I asked.

"I want Contemptible Blue to eat me up."

"Why?"

"Well, I've lived a long life. I've loved and learned enough for one lifetime. But the past few year have been cruel to me. My wife and my children all succumbed to ocean madness. They're gone now, and I'm old. I'm so very old, Captain. Old and tired. I'm ready to die, that much is certain, but I do not wish to go out the same way my loved ones went—slowly, painfully and without dignity. No, Captain, I want to die a beautiful death, or as close to such a thing as there is. I want to be eaten by Contemptible Blue, the foremost natural wonder of the Earth. I'll accept no other death."

"Awww, heeeeey, come ooooooon, buddy," I said, doing the bare minimum at trying to talk him out of suicide. "Come oooon. Nooo, man. Heeey. Stoooop."

"No use in trying to talk me out of it," Sebastian said.

"Well, alright," I said, happy I didn't have to put on that little show anymore.

"So can you lead me to Contemptible Blue? Please, Captain," he said.

"People pay me *good* money to hunt whales. I can find Contemptible Blue, but it'll cost you," I bluffed, hoping the fisherman didn't know people don't get paid to whale.

"I am the poorest living soul on the planet," he said.

"No money, no whaley."

"Well, all right then. Will you spear me through the head with this harpoon?"

"Yeah sure."

I was about to do the job but then Sebastian got too scared and backed out of the suicide-by-harpoon plan, so instead we just kept chatting.

"So you really wish to kill him, don't you?" Sebastian asked me. "That is why you got shipwrecked, I suppose? That's why I found you stranded in the middle of the ocean. He destroyed your ship, yes?"

"Well technically *I* lit the dynamite. It's kind of a long story. So one day my therapist told me to read *Moby Dick* and—" I began to explain, excited to tell the long, complicated story from the beginning.

"You whalers never learn," Sebastian interrupted. "You refuse to accept your place in the world. You think you can rewrite God's plan. Think you can conquer the unconquerable. You can't, son. God didn't make Contemptible Blue to be killed. You're smaller than you're willing to accept."

"I'm taller than *you,*" I shot back, even though Sebastian was significantly taller than me.

Like, two-and-a-half feet taller.

Sebastian told me he needed to sail back to shore for supplies. I went off to bed while he steered us north to the closest port. As I lay in bed, I thought long and hard about what Sebastian had said—about knowing and accepting one's place in the world, and for a moment I thought that maybe conquering something bigger than myself *wouldn't* bring me happiness. I thought about going back to land and settling down, maybe meeting a nice girl and starting a family. Then I remembered my sea siren dream and I decided to stay being a whaler. "Definitely gonna get back into it," I told myself.

XXVII.

There Is A Gigantic Hole Inside Of Me

Sebastian docked his sailboat at the wharves in a seaside town called Kurd. While he shopped for supplies, I went and took a little walk around. It was a quiet, cozy place, bustling with a lot of simple-living townie families. It reminded me of Skalego, because I hated it. I found a tavern and went in there to kill time before returning to the sea with Sebastian, who said I could tag along when he shipped back out to sea to take another stab at the suicide-by-whale thing.

I took a seat at the bar and the bartender greeted me warmly. "Good morning, lad. My name is Copernicus, like the astrologer."

"I haven't met him. Let me get a small beer," I said. "It was the drink of choice of an old friend of mine."

"Be ye a man of the navy?" the bartender asked me.

"No, just a humble, lowly, muscular whaler."

"Oh, all right. 'Cause drinks are free for men of the navy."

"Actually you know what though? I'm

actually just remembering that actually I *am* in the navy. I forgot I was in there."

"One small beer coming up, on the house."

"Sick!!!"

Also, real quick: at that same moment, two women came into the tavern and sat at the bar and one of the women said to the other one, "Nice weather, huh?"

"Yes," the other woman said.

Continuing on with my Bechdel Test-passing story: I sat and drank my free small beer and chatted with the bartender about life in Kurd. I tried to slip some stuff about being in the navy in there, too. "So, what do people do for work around here?" I asked. "Do people have jobs, like how I do the navy?"

"Yes, of course," said the bartender. "We're a small town, as ye've surely noticed. Many retired whalers call Kurd home. We attract a lot of tourists, too. Many of us Kurdians work in the tourism industry, givin' tours and selling souvenirs, for Kurd is home to the world's largest whaling museum." The phrase "whaling museum" seriously almost made me hurl. I was literally about to retch. The bartender was lucky I didn't freaking spew all over his bar.

I drank for hours, on the house, and told the bartender about how I used to be a whaler and still had a lot of regrets about failing to kill my big target, Contemptible Blue.

"Ahh, yes," said the bartender, "I've heard the tales of the great Contemptible Blue. They say he can't be hunted. But no whaler can be blamed for tryin'. Just think of the payday—the barrels and barrels of whale oil he'd supply ye. The hundreds and hundreds of oil lamps he'd fuel, the thousands and thousands of pounds of soap."

I didn't know whales could be used for things. I thought whaling was strictly recreational.

"I guess I just feel like... I don't know, like

there's a gigantic hole inside me," I confessed to the bartender, "and the only thing that could plug such a big hole is something just as big as the hole itself. Like Contemptible Blue."

"Well, ye're a man of the navy, and ye oughta be proud."

"No I'm not," I said, forgetting about the navy lie.

"I know," the bartender admitted. "I could tell ye weren't, but ye looked like ye needed a drink, on the house. Captain Fortnight, my lad, have ye tried lookin' to God to fill that hole in your heart?"

"I don't believe in God."

"What *do* ye believe in, lad?"

"I have absolutely no idea."

I tried to order another round, but the bartender said I had to start paying. "Unbelievable," I said as I stormed out. I paced around the streets for a little while and then went and threw rocks at the whaling museum.

Later, I met back up with Sebastian the sad sailor at the wharf, where he was loading up his sailboat. "Ahoy, Captain Stupid Idiot Who Fucked Up and Blew Up His Friend," he greeted me. "Are you ready to ship? I've got a whale to hunt, and subsequently get eaten by. The sweet release of death awaits me on the water."

"Sebastian, can I be honest with you? You're bumming me out," I said.

"I know," Sebastian said sadly. "Don't fret, my friend, for I'll be dead soon."

"See, that's the thing, is you keep talking about your suicide," I said.

"I understand," said Sebastian. "But, I'll be whale food very soon, so you won't have to deal with me much longer, my friend."

"See, you keep doing that, and it makes other people uncomfortable," I said.

"Yes. I apologize if it lowers your spirits. At least I'll be chewed to death by a whale soon, and it shall no longer be your problem," Sebastian said.

"You just... you just *keep* doing it," I said.

"Yes, sorry, I must not be pleasant company, but look on the bright side: I'm committing suicide-by-whale very soon, and you'll never have to deal with me again."

"Okay, well, I can tell you're just gonna keep doing this, so let's change the subject."

"Yes, let's change the subject to something lighter, for it might be nice to have a pleasant chat before I hurl myself into the ocean and swim directly into a whale's mouth and get eaten to death."

"Okay fuck this," I said before finally ditching Sebastian.

I wandered around Kurd for hours and

hours feeling lost and bored, glaring with contempt at all the townie couples with their kids laughing and smiling as they walked. They must have been so miserable. I couldn't bear to go back out to sea with Sebastian the mopey fisherman, so there I was, stuck on land, miles and miles away from prime whaling territory with no plan. I felt completely empty and without purpose. I began to wonder if Sebastian had the right idea. "He does," I eventually decided. Then I ran back to the wharf to try and catch up with him and join the suicide-by-whale mission, but by the time I made it there he'd already set sail. I saluted the sea and said, "May you die very soon, Sebastian," just trying to put positive vibes out into the universe for Sebastian.

I thought long and hard about the past weeks—about what a failure they'd been—and wondered what *else* I could do with myself to make myself feel whole. Maybe climb a mountain or try to seduce the president or get into stand-up. But, eventually, I concluded that I was doomed to feel this way forever, just like any other rational man who stops to ponder the human condition for more than 30 seconds.

"I give up," I whispered to the sea. "You win. I lose. I'm nothing. Long live Contemptible Blue."

XXVIII.
Beowulf

Officially retired from whaling, I spent the next ten years living a gigantic lie that wore down my soul little by little until I felt like the smallest living thing on the planet. Even smaller than a toad, the smallest conceivable thing.

I settled down in Kurd and lived the honest life of a retiree. I rented a small room in the upstairs of a local tavern and got a job as a salesman at the local harpoon store. I worked on the showroom floor, slinging harpoons to whalers, telling them things like, "This is a great model here. You got a real nice, sturdy shank on this guy. But if you're serious about whaling, you might be better off with a two-flue model. I'd suggest the HP-16002F. Hell of a harpoon for the price. You're lookin' at a nice 150-foot line length on this one, and a nice sealskin binding. Real good bang for your buck. Hell of a harpoon."

I tried to make peace with civilian life and avoid thinking about my whaling past, but every time I sold a harpoon at work, I secretly hoped that it was the harpoon that would one day be used by some brave whaler to kill Contemptible Blue. It'd be nice to know my product was being used for good.

I changed my name from Captain Fortnight to Beowulf. I figured that if I was going to live a painfully average, typical life, I should just have a typical name too.

I tried to take up fishing as a hobby, because that's what everyone else in town did with their spare time, but in ten years I didn't catch anything but a bunch of old boots. (There was a boot factory in Kurd with questionable waste disposal practices.) In the evenings I kept myself occupied by refurbishing all the old boots I caught while fishing. On the weekends I'd set up a little booth on Main Street and try to sell my refurbished boots, but no one bought a single one, let alone a pair.

I joined a book club because I thought it would be a nice way to make friends in town and stay busy, but I quit immediately when I found out we were reading *Moby Dick*. I just couldn't bear it —it reminded me too much of Contemptible Blue. Plus the book's bad.

I tried getting into stand-up comedy as a

hobby, even though my co-workers were always telling me I should never try stand-up. I figured I had a pretty good story to tell. I'd go to local open mics in Kurd a couple nights a week and do some of my stuff. "You know how sometimes you be on a boat, right?" I'd joke, "and everything's going good—right?—and you're thinking, 'Alright I got this, I'm good,' and then all of a sudden, you accidentally blow the boat up with dynamite and your buddy Kragg dies?" I never really got any laughs. I think my stuff was too alt for mainstream crowds.

I tried getting into the local dating scene. There were a lot of single women in Kurd, because a good portion of the men in town were married to the sea. Literally, you could legally marry the sea in Kurd. But in ten years, I never got a second date. Finally, I gave up on finding love and got married to the sea like all the other guys in town. *Welp, never gonna have sex again,* I thought to myself.

I felt so boring, so ordinary—just a guy named Beowulf who sold harpoons and was legally married to a body of water. Can you even imagine a more cliched life?

I tried and tried to accept the civilian's life, but every night, just as I'd begin to drift off to sleep, images of Contemptible Blue would flash in my head. I couldn't sleep. I'd toss and turn all night until the sun came up, and it was time once again to go sell harpoons. The ol' nine to five for the rest of my life.

I spent a lot of my time in Kurd thinking about mortality, and realized that Kragg never got the proper funeral he deserved. *Better late than never*, I thought to myself. I made a little person that kind of resembled Kragg out of a burlap sack and some leaves and held a proper funeral. I figured he'd want to be buried rather than cremated, since cremation was basically his cause of death.

"What can I say about Kragg?" I said as I lowered him into the ground, eulogizing my late friend. "He died the way he lived—alone and without a face. Poor Kragg perished trying to find his stepbrother Captain Blagg, who also died at sea. But I like to think that Kragg and Captain Blagg have been reunited now—maybe their bones washed up on the same beach or something, just coincidentally. It's nice to think about. Rest in peace, big guy. Maybe it's a coincidence, but I haven't had a good day since you died."

XXIX.

The 15th Annual Kurd Clams N' Shanties Seaside Festival

It was the first day of the 15th Annual Kurd Clams N' Shanties Seaside Festival. The Annual Kurd Clams N' Shanties Seaside Festival was a festival that happened in Kurd annually. This was the 15th one.

On Main Street, local artisans and merchants of all types would set up booths and sell their work, like figurines they'd whittled out of driftwood or ocean landscapes they'd painted. Local cooks would set up booths of their own, serving up steamed clams, fried shrimp and other homecooked seafoods. I had a booth of my own, too, selling my refurbished boots. Sales were low, even though I was offering a pretty good deal: buy one boot, get the other one free.

The whole ordeal was like an assault on all

my senses. The sight of the schlubby townies sweating bullets in their booths, the smell of clams baking in the hot summer sun, the sound of people telling me no when I'd try to sell them on my boots, the taste of failure, the feeling of crushing, all-encompassing emptiness. Just a salty, sweaty nightmare disguised as neighborliness. A painful reminder that another year of my life had slipped away from me.

Every year during the Annual Kurd Clams N' Shanties Seaside Festival, taverns all across town would book singers to come sing sea shanties. While I was manning my boot booth there on Main Street, I spotted a flier hung on a nearby gas light that read: "Your Worst Night-Maritime, 8:00 P.M. live @ Chadwick's Tavern." Right there on the flier was a picture of an old familiar face. It was my ex-bandmate Abbadon, the cowardly sailor-turned-rockstar from The S.S. Captain Fortnight's Big Boat days. He was still touring with Your Worst Night-Maritime, playing sea shanties that *I* helped pen.

I tore the flier off the pole and ripped it into shreds. I was furious and desperately needed to blow off some steam. I put a foot through my own booth, kicking it to pieces, then I took all my refurbished boots and chucked them at the ocean, which was technically spousal abuse. I was still pissed off, and eventually I just flew off the handle completely, kicking all the other Kurdians' booths to pieces too. "Beowulf!" yelled Troy, a local Kurdian who had a booth selling all the rocks he'd found around town that kind of resembled fishes. "Have ye gone mad, lad? Ye're spoilin' the 15th Annual Kurd Clams N' Shanties Seaside Festival!"

"Yeah, well, *fuck* the 15th Annual Kurd Clams N' Shanties Seaside Festival!" I yelled. "And you know what? Fuck the *14th* Annual Kurd Clams N' Shanties Seaside Festival! While we're at it, fuck the *13th* Annual Kurd Clams N' Shanties

Seaside Festival. I'll even go so far as to say fuck the *12th* Annual Kurd Clams N' Shanties Seaside Festival. And the *11th* Annual Kurd Clams N' Shanties Seaside Festival? What a *bust* that one was. *Fuck* the 11th Annual Kurd Clams N' Shanties Seaside Festival. And you know what else? I'm just gonna come out and say it, 'cause I *know* no one else has the balls: fuck the *10th* Annual Kurd Clams N' Shanties Seaside Festival. And can we talk about the *9th* Annual Kurd Clams N' Shanties Seaside Festival for a minute please? What a horseshit year that was. Fuck the 9th Annual Kurd Clams N' Shanties Seaside Festival. And you know what? I'm gonna make some enemies with this one, but I *gotta* get this off my chest: fuck the 8th Annual Kurd Clams N' Shanties Seaside Festival. I mean, am I the bad guy here? And since we're laying it all out on the table here, can I just say: fuck the 7th Annual Kurd Clams N' Shanties Seaside Festival. The 6th Annual Kurd

Clams N' Shanties Seaside Festival was a nightmare and I feel like *noone's* talking about it. Let's just be real here: fuck the 6th Annual Kurd Clams N' Shanties Seaside Festival. Fuck the 5th Annual Kurd Clams N' Shanties Seaside Festival, too. I didn't live here for the 4th, 3rd, 2nd or 1st Annual Kurd Clams N' Shanties Seaside Festivals, but fuck those ones. Oh, and *fuck you*, Troy."

"Hey, fuck you," said Troy.

"Fuck you dude," I responded.

"Yeah, well, fuck you too," Troy suggested.

"No, fuck *you*, actually," I countered.

"You know what, man? Fuck you," Troy quipped.

"Well, fuck you," I soliloquized.

"Fuck you," proposed Troy.

"Shut up Troy," I said, addressing Troy's point.

"*You* shut up," Troy put forward.

"Oh, *fuck* you," I concluded.

Contemptible Blue

I guess I had ten years of repressed rage to blow off. I definitely ruined the 15th Annual Kurd Clams N' Shanties Seaside Festival. I wasn't proud of myself. After my outburst, all of Main Street was littered with my wreckage—trampled handcrafts, torn up artwork and spoiled food. The local cooks struggled to pry their steamed clams out from between the cracks of the cobblestone street.

After ten years of trying to just blend in and be a civilian, I had made myself the town pariah with one quick outburst. With nothing left to lose, I stormed off to go confront Abbadon. "The town name rhymes with '*turd*'!" I pointed out to the Kurdians as I stormed off, getting one last blow in. I had been holding that in for ten years. "He's right," I heard someone whisper sadly.

XXX.

HP-20003F

I darted over to the harpoon store I worked at, let myself in and grabbed the most powerful weapon we had for sale: the HP-20003F harpoon *gun.* The HP-20003F was a real nice model. We're talkin' a 100% hickory shaft with a nice, sturdy endblade, not to mention a three-flue design, which was an industry first. Plus, you're lookin' at a tarred hemp line with a 250-foot reach. Just a real nice harpoon. Hell of a model.

It was nearly 7:45 P.M. and Your Worst Night-Maritime would soon be hitting the stage at Chadwick's Tavern. On my way there I felt a familiar feeling—an exhilarating sense of being on the hunt again. I hadn't had that feeling since being on the hunt for Contemptible Blue ten years ago. I had failed at that mission, but it would be much easier to harpoon a human being at close range, *especially* with the HP-20003F harpoon gun. Harpoon Nut magazine named it the best harpoon gun model of the year. Just a real nice harpoon, all around. Lowest frequency of line breakage of any model on the market. Just a beautiful piece of equipment.

"Let's do this thing!" I said as I walked, all psyched to go harpoon a guy.

I busted into Chadwick's Tavern and up there on stage was Abbadon, backed by his 12-piece band. They were in the middle of playing "Throw Away The Stowaway," which was not only *my* song, but also, for the most part, my only achievement at that point in my life. Chadwick's Tavern was packed and the crowd was loving the shanties. I loomed in the back of the room, watching the band play and listening to the sound of betrayal in musical form. Finally, when enough was enough, I took a deep breath, aimed my harpoon gun and fired at Abbadon, but I missed and the harpoon shot through the drummer's bass drum. I fired off another harpoon and almost took out the fife player. The band scattered and security rushed in, threw me back out onto the street and confiscated my harpoon. Of the dozens of harpoons I've had confiscated from me in my lifetime, the HP-20003F was the hardest to part with.

"I make more money in an hour than you make in a *year*," I yelled to the security guard, lying.

Security loomed by the front entrance to make sure I didn't try to get back in. I could hear the band begin to start up again. They played a few more shanties, then I heard Abbadon say, "Goodnight Kurd! We've been Your Worst Night-Maritime! I came up with the name!"

"No he didn't!" I yelled from outside.

I sneaked around to the back of the tavern and waited. After a few hours, a very drunk

Contemptible Blue

Abbadon and his many bandmates stumbled out the back door of the tavern and began loading their instruments into their tour carriage. A swarm of attractive, female groupies trailed behind them. That's the rock n' roll lifestyle of a sea shanty writer.

I rushed Abbadon and tackled him to the ground. His bandmates ran over and tried to pull me off. "Get your grubby little hands off me!" I told them. I try to never use the word "grubby" lightly, so you *know* I must have been pissed off.

"You!" Abbadon cried, my hands still around his neck. "I remember thy face, thou aged seaman! Thou art Captain Fortnight!"

"That's right, Abba*dick*!" I said. I *don't* swap the syllables of people's names out with the word "dick" lightly. I guess I *do* do it pretty often, but don't let that make you think this wasn't serious.

"Captain!" Abbadon pleaded. "Wast it *thy*

harpoon I only narrowly dodged on stage tonight?"

"That's right!" I admitted. "You've been making a lavish living off sea shanties that *I* helped write! Your Worst Night-Maritime was e*verything* to me, for a few days ten years ago."

"Twas't my assumption, Captain, that thyself and thy crew hadst certainly perished at sea! I could fathom no other ending! Captain, hear thee my plea: I made a small fortune playing this gig tonight, regaling these simple locals with my beautiful sea shanties. Please, let me taketh thee out and treat thee to a splendid evening! It shall be my manner of apologizing!"

"Fine, but watch yourself, *Crap*adon," I said. Admittedly, the "Crapadon" bit was way too harsh. There was no excuse for that, no matter how mad I was. Just absolutely brutal.

Abbadon took me to the hottest nightclub in all of Kurd, The Seamen Hole. I laughed at the funny tavern name for a while and then we went in there. Abbadon asked what was so funny but I didn't bother to explain because I've always had a sophisticated sense of humor that a lot of people don't get.

It was past midnight now, but the party was still raging at The Seamen Hole—the Clams N' Shanties Seaside Festival *always* kept the locals raging. Abbadon had a private VIP room, complete with bottle service. A bunch of Your Worst Night-Maritime groupies were back there drinking and getting wild. Abbadon and I took a seat and Abbadon ordered us a bottle of top-shelf brandy. The heavy upright-bass of the sea shanties shook the whole venue while the strobe gas lights flashed and the ladies danced. It was a wild scene. "Wow, you're really *doing* it, huh?" I said to Abbadon.

"I suppose I am, Captain Fortnight," he said.

"You're *really* livin' the rockstar life, man,"

I said.

"I suppose so, my dear friend. Aye, I am a blessed man, my heart full of gratitude, for I am fortunate to hath led a life so enchanted," Abbadon said modestly.

"Look at all these beautiful women," I remarked.

"Aye!" said Abbadon. "It is just as they always sayeth, Captain Fortnight: if the shanties are hot, the panties will drop."

"What the fuck?"

I got good and drunk off free brandy courtesy of Abbadon and tried to avoid any questioning about my new life in Kurd, but eventually Abbadon came out and asked, "Art there any women in thy life?

"I'm married," I said.

"Congratulations! Who is the lucky lass?" Abbadon asked.

"The ocean."

"Oh... Well that's..."

"Yeah..."

"That's great, Fortnight..."

"Yeah..."

"Well, you know, congratulations."

"Yeah, thanks."

"Yeah, man."

"Yeah... Cool..."

Abbadon went on to ask me what became of the crew of The S.S. Captain Fortnight's Big Boat after he abandoned the voyage. "That was a grim time," I said solemnly. "The whole crew died shortly after you fled. Kragg, Dr. Moseley, Egbert, Wigmund, Aldous, Milton, Bartleby, Langdon, Norman and Reginald—they all met their fate on the high seas. I'm the only one who survived, if you can call what I'm doing now 'living.'"

"Let us both enjoy a shot of whiskey in honor of each man lost," Abbadon proposed. He ordered ten shots for each of us and after drinking my share, as well as some of Abbadon's while he was in the bathroom, I was getting drunk and pretty emotional.

"I'm not even really a captain, man," I confessed drunkenly to Abbadon. "I had never even been on a boat before that voyage. I just read a few pages of *Moby Dick* and thought it sounded easy. Now I'm just a *stupid* harpoon salesman with a large body of water for a wife."

"Indeed I *wast* curious why thy life had become so suspiciously sealess—why thou hath settled down on dry land in Kurd," Abbadon said. "Be thee not ashamed of quitting the whaling life, for certainly we both remember that I too quit the sea because I wast afraid of fish."

Abbadon and I finally hugged it out. "It's okay to cry," he told me as we embraced in our hug.

"That's okay," I said. "Look Abbadon, I

don't say this to people as often as I should, but I'm sorry I tried to shoot you with a harpoon gun."

By now, the sexy lady groupies had gotten uncomfortable with all the hugging and crying and had left. "Hear me, Captain Fortnight," Abbadon sniffled.

"It's Beowulf now," I said, completely humiliated.

"I knew thee as 'Captain' ten years ago, and it is as so that I knoweth thee now. Captain, if thy life on dry land hath brought greater misery than thy life at sea, why not simply return to the sea once again?"

"Oh, I could never—"

"Nonsense! Hordes of famed whalers reside only 15 miles north of here, in the sea swept town of Cape Mueller. I am friendly with a lauded crew of whalers there who call themselves The Unsinkable Sixty. They are the largest crew of whalers ever assembled, and the most renowned.

Every green seaman with hopes of becoming a whaler harbors more pressing hopes of joining this crew, for there is none more competent. I am confident this crew of burly braves would bring thee aboard as an ordinary seaman if thy allegiance was solemnly pledged. Whaling season begins in 30 days, Captain, and it is not a far trek."

"I don't know..."

"Captain, strike me dead if I am being too bold, but it is my steadfast belief that thou shalt never find happiness until thy sworn personal promise is upheld—to strike dead Contemptible Blue. Consider it, Captain, and be thee not afraid of the sea. It hath been a tremendous joy to see thee tonight."

"You too, Abbadon. I know I've already said it a million times tonight, but I'm really sorry again about the 'Crapadon' thing."

"All right," Abbadon said. "Now if thou wilt excuse me, I must go catch up with those

ladies, for I intend to do a *different* kind of fishin'
tonight, if thou knoweth what I mean."

"Dude, what the *fuck?*"

Abbadon the pervert ran off to find the
ladies and I left The Seamen Hole drunk, alone and
with my mind racing. I stumbled home and
crawled into bed, thinking about everything
Abbadon told me. He'd followed his dreams and
made it work, against all odds. If a cowardly sailor
who's afraid of fish can reinvent himself as a
rockstar sea shanty singer, then surely I could hunt
a whale. I had nothing to lose. I was *already* the
town loser. I couldn't think of any reason *not* to go
to Cape Mueller, beg for a job on a whaleship and
sail off once again into the treacherous blue yonder
with a bunch of strange men.

Contemptible Blue

XXXI.

30 Days 'Til Whaling Season

I had 30 days to prepare before whaling season—before heading off to Cape Mueller to track down The Unsinkable Sixty, the best crew in the entire world. Alongside them, I'd kill Contemptible Blue, or *die* trying. Either one would be fine.

I didn't have much time to get into whaling shape, so I had to act fast. First, I went to Kurd Library and stole a copy of *Moby Dick* again. I needed to rediscover my inspiration. I got a quarter of the way through it this time, and I truly did not understand a word of it, so I went back and got a new book called *Grasping Dick* (grow up!), a guide to interpreting *Moby Dick*, but I didn't understand that book either so I went back again and got *The Grasping Dick Companion*, a guide to interpreting *Grasping Dick*. Then I decided I was wasting too much time reading.

I needed to bone up on my harpoon skills. I spent every day at the local harpoon range, shooting at a stationary target with my harpoon gun. The first few days I didn't hit the target a single time, plus I accidentally took out a few employees, but by week two of training I was shooting with 50% accuracy. By week three, I was hitting my target every time. It turns out that when I focused on it, I was actually a natural at shooting things with a harpoon. By week four I was even doing trick shots. I could shoot behind my back and even through my legs. Right handed, left handed, with my eyes closed—I could do it all. I had this funny trick shot I'd do where I'd pretend to check my watch on the hand I was holding the harpoon with, then I'd casually shoot the harpoon gun and pretend like it was an accident. A lot of people moved out of Kurd when they heard how good I was getting at shooting things with a harpoon gun. The town population dropped 33%.

I put myself on an all fish diet to become accustomed to the sailor's diet. In order to prepare myself for several months at sea with no sex, I continued to not have sex.

I felt myself growing more seaworthy every day. The fire was back. I was ready to finish what I started ten years earlier—to reduce Contemptible Blue to a bloody glob of guts and blubber in the middle of the ocean. On day 28, I put on my old monkey jacket and began the long walk over to Cape Mueller to track down The Unsinkable Sixty. On the way, I felt something in the pocket of my monkey jacket. It was the old, charred badge of Captain Meierhorn, that old Confederacy for the War on Whalers captain that I blew up. "Ha ha, that was crazy," I chuckled to myself. I hadn't thought about it in a while. "That guy was fucked up."

Things needed to be different this go-around. "No violence this time," I promised myself. I checked my watch to make sure I was making good time but then muscle memory kicked in from doing my checking-the-watch trick shot and I accidentally fired my harpoon gun and took out a mailman. "No violence starting *now*," I told myself.

Before leaving, I'd spent a few days tightening up my nautical resume so I could land that job with The Unsinkable Sixty.

Captain Fortnight

Nautical Professional

254 Anchor Pl.

Town of Kurd, U.S.

Objective:

Seeking a challenging and fulfilling career in the whaling arts

Education:

No

Experience:

Fishy Al's Harpoon Depot | Salesperson

- Primarily sell harpoons and replacement harpoon parts
- Maintain thorough knowledge of new trends in harpoon technology
- Upsell warranties and harpoon accessories to maximize profit

- Placed 12th in this month's Employee of the Month ballot

SS Captain Fortnight's Big Boat | Whaler

- Responsible for overseeing operations aboard
- Responsible for spotting and hunting whales
- Successfully survived shipwreck that killed 12 people

Confederacy for the War on Whalers | Deck Hand

- Successfully blew up the entire Confederacy with dynamite

References

No

SMALL BRIBE AVAILABE UPON REQUEST

XXXII.

A Mere Canaller In A Nantucketer's Clothing

After a day of travel I finally reached the town of Cape Mueller on the eve of the first day of whaling season. I spotted a small map store and went in to ask one of the map salesmen for directions to the wharves. Then he tried to sell me a map. That's how those map salesmen get you. "Name's Frank, by the way. Welcome to Cape Mueller," the map salesman told me.

I finally caved and bought a map from Frank the virgin. "Ah yes, a map," I said. "I should have no trouble reading this."

I tried to follow the map to the local wharf and ten minutes later I was somewhere in the jungle stuck in quicksand. There must have been something wrong with the map. I would have to be sure to press charges against that map salesman after I finished killing my whale.

Contemptible Blue

I managed to escape the jungle and retrace my steps back to Cape Mueller, and then I happened upon the wharves. Before going over there, I stopped to have a private moment with my wife, the ocean, to say goodbye before sailing out. I knelt down and said to her, "Hey honey, it's CF. I think you should know, because I don't want any secrets between us, that I tried very, very hard to cheat on you several times. Nothing ever happened, I swear, but I really tried. I really was out there every single night trying to make that happen. If the opportunity had come up, I would have taken it, for sure. No questions asked. I truly would have said yes to any sexual advance from any woman. I just want to get that off my chest, in case I die on this trip, which I probably will. Also, let's divorce."

Rows and rows of whaleships lined the shore. Every crew in town was loading their ship and preparing to ship out. "Here I come!" I yelled aloud confidently as I approached the wharf. "Alright," someone yelled back.

I approached the biggest, bravest looking crew I could find. They were loading cargo on a ship called The Poseidon. It must have been named after the captain's kid or some shit. I approached one of the crew members, who was sitting on a crate splicing a rope, and asked him if he knew where I could find The Unsinkable Sixty. "Ye're lookin' at 'em," he said.

"Great," I said, "I'm looking for a job on a whaleship. Please allow me to—wait, you don't drug test, right?"

"No."

"Great. Allow me to give you a copy of my resume. And let me be upfront: I have several weaknesses. Number one: sometimes I care *too* much. Number two: sometimes I work *too* hard," I said. This was a classic job interview trick—frame your weaknesses as strengths. "Number three—" I continued.

"Have ye any experience on a whaleship?" the guy asked, cutting me off. I was glad he cut me off because I couldn't think of any more flattering weaknesses and I almost started listing real weaknesses on accident, like how I was responsible for all those deaths.

"You'll see on my resume that I have extensive—" I began to say.

"Yay or nay, chowder head?" he asked. This guy was really preying on my insecurities—I'd always worried that people were calling me "chowder head" behind my back. I had to let it go and carry on. "Yes, I've whaled before," I said.

"Under the command of which captain?" asked the crewman.

"Yours truly, baby."

"What's yer name?"

"Captain Fortnight."

"I've not heard of ye. But if ye want a job,

we need swabbies—mere ordinary seamen, the lowest ranking of all the crew. Ye'll get the 715th lay, so upon returning to the shore after the voyage, ye'll pocket about ten dollars."

"You get *paid* for this!?" I said, stunned.

"Yes, of course," he said, sounding kind of confused.

"Unreal. Anyway, killing Contemptible Blue would've been payment enough."

"*Kill* Contemptible Blue? Are ye jokin', lad?"

"No. If I was joking, *you'd* be laughing. That reminds me: you know how sometimes you be on a whaleship, right?" I said, launching into some of my material, "and you accidentally blow up the entire—"

"I don't have time for this," the crew member heckled. "But I do enjoy an ordinary seaman with a sense of humor. Ye gotta have a sense of humor in that line of work, for the pay is little and the work is thankless."

I began to have second thoughts. I was not aware that no one would be thanking me for cleaning the boat. *That's fucked up*, I thought. I accepted nevertheless. "I want the job," I said.

"Lad, I am only a mere ordinary seaman meself. Ye'll need to speak with the captain. I'll fetch him."

The ordinary seaman wandered off and came back a few minutes later with the captain, a statuesque blonde young man who sized me up stoically and then asked, "Are ye fit for the sea, or be ye some mere Buffalonion canaller in a Nantucketer's clothing?" The whole crew laughed at the captain's joke. Luckily I have a pretty good sense of humor about myself so I was able to laugh about it too. "Ha ha, you got me," I said. "Anyway," I continued, "I *am* fit for the sea. First, here are my weaknesses. Number one: sometimes I care *too* much. Number two: I'm responsible for the deaths of several sai—I mean, I work too hard. Number three—"

"Ye stand tall and puff yer chest, but ye've the countenance of a mere shrimper!" the captain said. The whole crew laughed again. I chuckled a little bit, too. "Ha ha, zinged me again," I admitted, being a good sport.

"I sure did, Captain *Fart*-night!"

"Oh, *FUCK* you."

I stormed off to go and find another crew, but the mean captain stopped me. "Not so fast, seaman! I was merely jestin'. Quit yer huffin' and make yer case: why should I let ye on me crew?"

"I'm friends with Abbadon," I said pleadingly.

"From Your Worst Night-Maritime?" the captain asked.

"Yeah!" I said.

"He fucked my wife."

"Oh..." I said awkwardly.

"Yeah..." the captain said after a long, uncomfortable silence.

"Alright, well..."

"Yeah..."

"I should just..."

"Yeah."

"Alright, well..."

"Right."

"Alright, well... Alright, I'm gonna split then."

"All right."

I walked off, leaving an awkward scene behind me, and then a sympathetic member of The Unsinkable Sixty pulled me aside and said, "Lad, I don't know if ye've already been made apprised of the matter, but 'tis not a good time to be a whaler. Not now, amid the great Blubber Rush. The whales are overfished and nigh impossible to come by, but if ye wish to carry forth, there's another crew of whalers right down the way. Rumor has it they need an ordinary seaman, for one of their men drowned last night. They call themselves The Blue Crew. But be ye warned, lad, their captain is a despotic leader and a lush, from what I hear. They say he's a hatred for Contemptible Blue that takes precedence over the safety of his crew. They say he's lost his marbles in his old age. Some say that to ship with The Blue Crew would be suicide. Their bond is weak, for there is a great division between the classes aboard their vessel. All feeling of brotherhood is tragically absent. Also, be ye aware, lad, that The Blue Crew are our rivals."

"Well, okay," I said, "I guess I'll go try to join The Blue Crew then."

"Very well, rival," the crew member said, then punched me in the stomach. "Blue Crew sucks!" he yelled.

I walked east towards where The Blue Crew were loading their ship. I decided to forego the interview process and just show up and pretend like I was already on the crew, which was the same way I got most of my jobs, like my old gig at the harpoon store or my brief stint as a mayor several years ago.

XXXIII.

The Blue Crew

The Blue Crew, too, were loading their ship for whaling season. Their ship was named The Vespertina. She was a little beat up, but still stood tall and proud, moored there at the wharf. Her three masts towered triumphantly over the decks, casting a long shadow over them. She doubled the size of the late S.S. Captain Fortnight's Big Boat and had way less holes in her sails. The crew was scrambling around, all looking like they had a job to do and knew how to do it well. Some guys loaded cargo while some swabbed the deck and others inspected the ship and scribbled down notes while others barked orders at the other guys. I went and picked up a box of rope and carried it a few feet and set it down, then picked it up and carried it back, pretending to be on the crew. Then I didn't know what else to do, so I pretended like I was one of the guys whose job it was to bark orders. "Swab the deck!" I yelled to no one in particular.

"*You,* ordinary seaman," someone yelled to me from up on the quarter deck, "quiet thy mouth! Load cargo!"

"Aye, aye, captain!" I said back. Then a tense, heavy hush came over the whole crew. Everyone froze and stared at me, looking horrified.

"*You,*" that same crew member said angrily, "did ye just address me as thy captain? Nay, I am *not* thy captain. I am the third mate, Paulo. Thy captain is Captain Wilhelm, and his gallantry, his poise, his sophistication dwarfs that of my own."

"I understand," I said. "You're second in command to Captain Wilhelm."

Contemptible Blue

The whole crew gasped yet again, and third mate Paulo looked furious. "How *dare* ye, ordinary seaman?" he snapped. "I am miles away from second in command! Have ye forgotten about thy second mate, Hobart?"

"Right, right," I said. "You're third in command after Captain Wilhelm and Hobart."

The whole crew gasped again. "Come on man!" someone yelled.

"Nay!" cried third mate Paulo. "I am not *third* in command, for the chief mate, Belmont, is ever my superior, his experience more vast, his heart more adamant, and his lust for the sea more profound."

Wow, that's one insecure third mate, I thought to myself. Maybe he was fat once.

Then some other guy, who looked just like Paulo but was slightly taller, appeared and joined Paulo's side up on the quarter deck. He pointed at me and said, "*You*, ordinary seaman, ye lowly worm, I am the second mate, Hobart. What's the trouble?"

"No trouble!" I insisted. "Just working hard!" Then I picked up that box of ropes and walked it around again. "The ol' nine to five!" I joked.

Then another guy, who also looked just like the first two guys but slightly taller, heard the commotion and joined them. "You there," he yelled at me, "I am Belmont, thy chief mate! Ye've rattled my fellow shipmates! What's the trouble?"

"No trouble, sir!" I yelled.

"Good!" chief mate Belmont said. Then Hobart, the second mate, dropped to his knees and began praising Belmont, the chief mate. "Ye've done a laudable job disciplining that foolish seaman," he said. "I'd follow thy lead come sunshine or tempest!"

"Thank you!" said chief mate Belmont. Then Paulo, the third mate, dropped to his knees and began praising Hobart, the second mate. "Thy respect for the chief mate is inspiring. I respect you," he praised.

"Thank you!" said Hobart.

These guys *really* respected rank. Personally, I never thought of "rank" as anything more than just a merit-based way of prioritizing people within a power structure, so I didn't really understand the big deal.

Then third mate Paulo yelled at me to load cargo. I went and helped the other lower-ranking seamen load cargo—fresh sails, foodstuffs, harpoons and tools. It was grunt work, but I was certain that I'd quickly rise up the ranks to become chief whaler, if that was a title that existed. If not, I'd be sure to create it. All the *best* job titles I'd had in the past had been ones I made for myself ("King of the Toilet Factory Assembly Line", "Grand Wizard of Janitorial Services", "Cowboy Mayor" etc.)

Soon, when all the prepping was done, third mate Paulo, second mate Hobart and chief mate Belmont positioned themselves up on the foredeck once again, lording over the rest of the crew, and prepared to address us.

"Ahoy, Blue Crew!" cried chief mate Belmont. The whole crew gave him our full attention.

"Great job getting the crew's attention," second mate Hobart whispered to chief mate Belmont. Then he turned to us and yelled, "That's right, men—listen to thy chief mate!"

"Hey, great job supporting chief mate Belmont back there," third mate Paulo whispered to second mate Hobart.

"Now then," continued chief mate Belmont, "The Vespertina is ready to ship. Take a glance around ye, men. Take a look at this kingly crew of hunters and bask!"

There I was, grouped with the ordinary

seamen, the poor losers of the crew. Just mere swabbies doing the dirty jobs. I was not among impressive company. All the ordinary seamen were dressed in tattered rags and looked sick, constantly wiping their snot off on their sleeves. A few of them were picking bugs out of each other's hair. I felt overqualified. I have a college degree, after all. It's not mine, but I have it.

Then there were the harpooners, the *coolest* guys on the crew. They were responsible for actually harpooning the whales. They were all muscly and handsome and had torn the sleeves off their monkey jackets and turned their fisherman's caps backwards. *Backwards!!!* The cool harpooners cracked jokes to each other and laughed while they smoked their pipes, looking like they didn't even *care* about the whaling voyage. They were all the same race, although I don't remember what it was right now. They ruled. *I GOTTA get in with that crew,* I thought to myself.

"What's up harpooners!?" I yelled over to them, trying to make friends. "I'll meet up with you guys later!"

"Shut up, ordinary seaman," one of them yelled back.

"Ha ha, classic!" I said. We had a pretty good rapport. "Y'all are wild!"

Then there was the small team of engineers, the guys who designed The Vespertina. They were total dorks with their hair impeccably middle-parted and their linen shirts tucked into high-waisted trousers. They were constantly scribbling down notes in their notebooks and pushing their glasses up on their noses. Me and my new friends on the harpoon team were *definitely* gonna give them hell, just as soon as the harpoon team realized I was cool and became my friends.

A small crew of carpenters reported to the engineers, along with a blacksmith and cooper. Our blacksmith was named Cooper and our cooper was named Black Smith. That was pretty funny.

Then there was the ship cook, Jojo. He was heavily tattooed, wearing a bandana, a thick five-o'-clock shadow and a tight-fitting wifebeater. He chain-smoked and paced around muttering to himself about his ex-wife. He had a weird energy. Standing near Jojo, there was also the ship steward. The steward's job was to help tend to the needs of the crew, serving their meals and cleaning up their messes. Our steward was named Herschel. He was a little boy. That was pretty much his whole thing. I even asked him if there was anything to him besides being a little boy and he said, "Aw gee whiz, mister, I don't know." So, being a little boy was basically his main shit.

The Blue Crew seemed pretty cliquey. It felt *just* like high school, I bet. I resented the idea of having to climb The Blue Crew social ladder in order to get ahead. I *hate* drama.

I broke off from the ordinary seamen and

tried to seamlessly integrate myself into the harpooner group. "*Pssst*, hey fellas, big prank on the engineer dorks tonight—you in?" I asked them.

"Get back yonder with the ordinary seamen!" one of them yelled, pushing me away.

"Ha ha, epic!" I said. "I'll catch up with you guys later!"

"*Enough!*" yelled chief mate Belmont from up on the foredeck of The Vespertina. "Thy chief mate is speaking!"

"Yeah!" yelled second mate Hobart. "Thy chief mate Belmont is speaking!"

"Yeah!" yelled third mate Paulo. "Listen to second mate Hobart—chief mate Belmont is speaking!"

I did a fake cough and muttered the word "loser!" under my breath, trying to make the harpooners laugh, but they didn't. I guess I didn't mutter it loud enough.

"You, my braves," chief mate Belmont

continued, "are here to man The Vespertina— this dashing, queenly craft—on a voyage that stands to make rich men of us all, so long as we know our roles, do them well and work together as brothers, for we shan't fetch a single drop of whale oil if we don't work together! To you greener seamen, all ye hopefuls who've never braved the sea afore: it *will* be hard. More often, it will be *hell*. Are ye ready to face the cold reality of the sea?"

"Here, here!" cheered the whole crew, except for me, who yelled, "Yeah, sounds good!" because I didn't know about the "Here, here!" thing.

"Then let us not loiter! Let us take to the sea, drain the riches from every passing whale and become wealthy men!" chief mate Belmont said.

"Here, here!" I cheered, but no one else did it this time. *What the fuck?*

Chief mate Belmont gave us all an approving nod and said, "Now we raise the anchor, set the sails and depart from this godforsaken wharf!" Then one of the cool harpooners did a fake cough and muttered, "Loser!" All the other harpooners started cracking up. "Ha ha ha, classic!" I said, joining in.

"Shut up, seaman," one of the harpooners said back.

"Enough!" chief mate Belmont insisted. "Any final questions before we ship out, thou confabulating fools!?" I raised my hand. "What's 'confabulating'?" I asked.

Some of my fellow ordinary seamen went off to raise the sails, second mate Hobart went and hoisted the anchor, and with that, I had finally returned once again to the sea. With nothing but clear skies above and an endless blue highway ahead, I felt alive again. "We're really doin' this thing!" I yelled triumphantly.

"Yeah!" one of the ordinary seamen yelled.

"Shut up!" I told him.

A few miles out, The Unsinkable Sixty, our rivals, came zipping past us in their ship The Poseidon. They already had a freshly killed whale in tow. As they passed, they pelted the side of our ship with tomatoes. "Blue Crew sucks!" they yelled.

"Ignore them!" chief mate Belmont insisted.

XXXIV.
Thar She Blows!

Once we were at sea I didn't really know what to do with myself so for a while I just walked around the main deck yelling "Thar she blows!" every couple of minutes until chief mate Belmont came out and asked me to stop, which was a relief because I was due for a break from working.

I approached one of my fellow ordinary

seamen and asked, "What should I be doing?"

"My brother," he said, "you need merely to remain alert and await your orders. Our shipmates will give them as needed. I am Dudley, by the way. How long have you been a seaman?"

"Well, it all began ten years ago. It's a long story. Okay, here goes: open on me reading a tattered old copy of *Moby Dick*. Smash cut to me at a harpoon store..." I said, excited to tell my whole story from the beginning.

"*Ten* years, and you are still a mere ordinary seaman?" interrupted Dudley.

"Listen, I've had a few setbacks. I'm *actually* a harpooner, like those boys over on the harpoon team. Where was I? Okay, so, dissolve to me meeting Kragg—"

"You need not explain yourself, nor do *any* of us ordinary seamen need to defend our rank, for there is no shame—no pitiable absence of honor—in being an ordinary seaman, my brother," Dudley interrupted again, "for we all must begin somewhere."

I wanted to make it clear to Dudley that I wasn't one of *them* so I pulled his pants down and I pointed at his penis and I yelled out, "If anyone wants to go fishin', here's a baby worm for ya!" A few of our fellow ordinary seamen laughed but the cool guys on the harpoon team ignored me. They must have been ignoring my funny joke as some sort of hazing ritual. It was a pretty cruel initiation, but I once ate a whole toilet to get into a fraternity, so I could handle it.

Dudley pulled his pants up and said, "Please brother, be a friend to me, as I will be the same to you. You needn't treat your fellow ordinary seamen in the same manner as those brutish harpooners. You are one of us by rank." Then he reached into his pocket, pulled out a small jar of some purplish fluid and took a big swig. I asked him what it was. "This is the healing nectar of the Eliki people," he said. "They are a small tribe of hunter-gatherers from the southern coast of Africa. On my first ever voyage, I saved one of the Elikis from drowning, for his legs had been chomped by the gaping maw of some dastardly whale. I was awarded a lifetime supply of this strange purple nectar as a show of gratitude. I know little of its ingredients, but I take a mere swig every day and I am healthy as an ox, never falling ill like many of my seafaring brethren. Here, brother, take a sip."

"Your lips were on it!" I yelled, swatting it out of his hands. "Now get lost. I'm gonna go say what's up to my boys on the harpoon team."

I ditched Dudley and went over and joined the harpooners, who were lazing about the quarter deck smoking, horsing around and sharpening their harpoons. "How's it hangin', fellas?" I asked, playing it cool. "What are you guys getting into tonight? Whatever it is, I'm down."

Contemptible Blue

The leader of the harpoon team, Darius, pulled my pants down, pointed at my penis and said to the other harpooners, "Hey boys, if any of thee wish to go fishin', I hath found a baby worm with which to bait thy hook." The rest of the guys started cracking up. They all high-fived and then ditched me on the quarter deck, pushing me aside as they went.

"Ha ha! You're a maniac, Darius!" I called out to them as they walked away. "I'll catch up with you guys later! If anyone wants to meet up and play catch on the foredeck later, I'm down!"

I went and re-joined the ordinary seamen to see what they were up to. I found them on the main deck, where they were all just standing around poking a dead fish with their fingers. Then they picked it up and started playing catch with it. They were a dirty, loathsome bunch, and I could hardly stand to be around them, but unfortunately there were no other options. The harpooners were still hazing me by pretending I wasn't funny, and the engineers were boring bookworms busy pacing around and scribbling into notebooks and muttering about the "questionable integrity" of the ship. The carpenters, cooper and blacksmith weren't really interested in hanging out. They just kind of sat around and catcalled nautical birds while awaiting orders from the engineers.

I approached the ordinary seamen and they asked me if I wanted in on their "game." I asked what the game was. "We are throwing a fish around," Dudley said, then he sneezed into his bare hands and wiped it off in his hair.

"Okay," I said, "I guess that's exactly what I thought you were doing. Bye."

I ditched the ordinary seamen and went and slumped over the aftmost bulwark to do some reflecting, peering into the open ocean behind me as we sailed along. I felt a hand on my shoulder. It was Dudley, who'd followed me. He was covered in fish guts.

"The fish exploded," he told me.

"Don't touch me," I insisted.

"You speak to me like my superior. Captain Fortnight, we are brothers, equal in rank. Why are you called 'captain' anyhow?"

"I was a captain once. You wouldn't understand, you're too stupid."

"But suppose the *real* captain, our eccentric, brooding Wilhelm with his alleged powder keg temper, heard you were being addressed by your fellow seamen as 'captain.' He'd have you tossed to sea."

I began to wonder about this Captain Wilhelm and why he hadn't shown his face yet. The Unsinkable Sixty had warned me that Captain Wilhelm was a tyrant, but I felt like I needed to meet the guy. When it benefits me, I'm pretty good at schmoozing authority. Plus, I had some suggestions for the captain on how to improve the crew, like how we could probably save money by firing the engineering team.

"Dudley," I said, "who is this Captain Wilhelm anyway?"

"Captain Wilhelm does not leave his stateroom except for under dire circumstances. When a whale is spotted and at last the great chase has come underway, he will emerge from below the decks, but not before then. Unless of course, my brother, it becomes necessary for the captain to administer his bloody brand of discipline unto an unruly crew member. If indeed you do find yourself face to face with the man, it means you have slighted him or his shipmates in some unforgivable way, which means, furthermore, your voyage is as good as over. You're best to leave him alone in his stateroom to his drinking and his mapping."

"Well I have a charismatic way of talking to people, Dudley," I said, "you dipshit. Where's his stateroom?"

Dudley led me to Captain Wilhelm's stateroom, which was hidden away in a sub-forecastle below the regular forecastle. The words "Do NOT disturb" were carved into the door. I guess it was for the housekeeping staff, which I didn't know we had. I went to knock on the door and Dudley grabbed my hand. "Seaman Fortnight, no, please," he said. "You shan't. Captain Wilhelm must not be disturbed. He will cut off that very hand with which you knock."

"It's fine, Dudley. I'm just gonna schmooze the captain a little bit. Just... go swab the deck!"

"We have only just set sail two hours ago. The deck is uncluttered and swabbed clean."

"Well, go raise the anchor."

"The anchor has been raised, Fortnight. We are at sea."

"Well, go batten the hatches, or whatever."

"The decks are bone dry. It is not necessary

to batten the—"

"Oh my god will you seriously please fuck off?"

Dudley finally left and then, just as I went to knock on the door of the captain's stateroom, I heard a low, grumbling voice bellow out from behind it: "I'll cut yer hands off."

"Lo siento!" I said, pretending to be housekeeping.

XXXV.

Captain Fortnight Talks To Jojo

I quickly went back above the decks and there I ran into Jojo, the twitchy, tattooed cook. He was on break, chain smoking and muttering about his ex-wife again. I tried to avoid him, but he cornered me into a conversation. He was hard to understand. He mumbled as he spoke and never made eye contact. He managed to tell me that he had fought in the war. "They really screwed us over there," I said, pretending to know which war he was talking about. Then he muttered something about his ex-wife again, and then said, clearly, "This is the only place on Earth a man can find peace—at sea, where there ain't no women to bother us. Just peace and quiet."

Herschel, the little boy steward, saw us and joined the conversation. "That's right!" Herschel said in agreement with Jojo. "No girls allowed out here! Just us men, doin' men's work! Now if you'll excuse me, I have to get back to my cleaning." Then I wandered off, thinking about how many men I had seen die since becoming a sailor.

XXXVI.

What's Up, My 'Pooners?

Later that night, as the sun went down after an uneventful day of smooth sailing, I went to go check in with the harpooners again to see if they wanted to chill. Hopefully the hazing ritual was over. They were up to their usual business, just hanging out on the quarter deck, sharpening their harpoons, doing pull-ups on the mizzenmast, smoking, talking about whales and women and doing general cool guy stuff. "What's up, my 'pooners!?" I greeted them. "Couple of 'poon hounds over here, am I right? Ha ha ha. Hell yeah. We hangin' our what, fellas?"

"Be gone," their leader Darius told me. "Toss thyself overboard, useless seaman. Thou art more useful as shark food!"

"Ha ha! You're a legend, Darius!" I said. "Woah, what's that you got there? Is that the

HPK2602F?" I asked one of the harpooners—I recognized his harpoon gun model from my days on the sales floor. "*Very* cool. Righteous line strength on that model. Oh, is that the HPJ14502F?" I asked another harpooner. "Excellent choice. Surprisingly lightweight for a bronze dart model. Definitely a solid harpoon you got there, my man. And that tarred hemp line? Get outta here—the best."

The boys looked impressed. "You, lowly seaman," Darius said, "what doth thou know about the sport of harpooning?"

"I'm a bit of a 'pooner myself. I used to whale back in the day."

"Tell me then, lowly seaman," Darius said, "what'st thy biggest conquest—thy biggest prize?"

"Uhh, ever hear of a little something called *Contemptible Blue*, my man?" I said. I could feel myself about to tell a big lie that might be hard to keep, and I knew I should cut myself off, but instead I doubled down. "I killed him," I said. "Yuuuup. I killed Contemptible Blue. 'Pooned him right between the eyes. Kapow! Killed him dead. Ask *anyone.* It's a known fact."

"Thou art a liar, and most certainly some sort of scoundrel," Darius said. "Even *we* know it to be true that Contemptible Blue can not be killed."

"Uhh, tell that to my *harpoon,*" I joked. A few of the guys chuckled. They were finally starting to realize I was cool.

"If thy tale is true, and thou art not simply a knave and a fool, then tell me, seaman: how long ago didst thou kill the famed leviathan?" Darius asked.

"Ten years ago today," I said, just pulling a number out of thin air.

"More lies! More scoundrelry! If thou hadst killed the famed blue leviathan ten years ago, The Confederacy for the War on Whalers would've blown thee to bloody bits, for they still policed the sea then."

"*I* blew up The Confederacy for the War on Whalers!" I squealed, excited to not be lying anymore.

"Dost thou think me some sort of imbecile?" Darius asked. "Dost thou see me as a mere brute, foolish enough to believe so queer a claim?"

"It's true!" I pleaded. "I blew them all up—Captain Meierhorn, his men, some asshole named Kragg—*all* of 'em." Then I reached into my pocket and flashed the charred badge of Captain Meierhorn. "Check it out, my man," I said. "See? It was me, Captain Fortnight."

Darius' eyes widened and his ears seemed to perk up. "Captain Fortnight," he repeated, looking like he was in deep recollection. "I recognize this moniker, for I hath sailed more tropical waters in my many countless years as a harpooner, and out near the sunny shores of the Galapagos I hath heard the parrots squawk this very name. 'Captain Fortnight set us free,' they would squawk."

"Oh yeah," I said, "Captain Meierhorn was friends with birds. I'm glad to hear they made it to the Galapagos. Anyway, next to ghostwriting songs for Your Worst Night-Maritime, blowing up The Confederacy is probably my best achievement."

"Your Worst Night-Maritime? They *rock.* Please pardon our dour disrespect," Darius said, then he grabbed me by the shoulders and clonked our two foreheads together in some sort of strange induction ceremony. "Thou art one of *us* now," he said. "Welcome to the tribe of tribes. A long life to thee, yes, and a merry death too. Please, join us. We were just trading tales of our adventures at sea."

"Right on, I'll chill," I said.

"How didst thou become a whaler?" one of

the harpooners asked me.

"Well, I leafed through *Moby Dick*, and it really changed my life. Made me realize it was the whaling life that I was meant to live," I said.

"Err... Did you read the ending?" one of them asked.

"Yeah!" I said, lying. "Crazy stuff. Anyway, wanna hear the story about how I killed Contemptible Blue again?" I asked.

"Yeah!" they agreed.

Me and my new harpooner friends stayed up all night, swapping stories about all our crazy adventures. As the moon rose higher and higher in the sky, I finally felt like I'd found my tribe. Down on the main deck below us, the ordinary seamen were comparing their scabs and boils. "Adios, losers," I whispered to myself as I watched them go about their gruesome business. "I'm cool now."

I noticed Dudley staring back at me from

down on the main deck. I saw a single tear roll down his cheek. I pointed it out to the rest of my boys on the harpoon team and we all started laughing and rippin' on Dudley. "The ordinary seaman is crying!" one of them said with a big, hearty laugh. "Ha ha ha!"

"Ha ha ha, Ugly Dudley!" I added. Oh my god, it was classic.

"It's okay to cry," I heard Dudley mutter to himself.

Later, third mate Paulo came around and told me and my fellow harpooners to "go bedward" for the night. He also chastised me for communing with the harpooners instead of my fellow ordinary seamen. "It's fine—the harpooners think I'm cool," I tried to explain, but he insisted I go re-join the ordinary seamen.

The ordinary seamen cabin was cramped and stunk of mold and rotten wood, not to mention the ordinary seamen themselves. When I got in there, all the ordinary seamen were reading scripture together. "Evening," Dudley greeted me. "Fortnight, we've just read a beautiful passage. Please, let me share it with you: 'Do not repay evil with evil or insult. On the contrary, repay evil with blessing, because to this you were called so that you may inherit a blessing."

"Fake!!!" I yelled.

Since we were pressed for space in the ordinary seamen quarters, we all had to sleep two seamen to a bed, so I made Dudley sleep on the floor so I could sleep solo in his bed. "It's only fair, for some reason," I argued.

"Fortnight, why must I slumber on the floor, with all its creaks and cracks? Please, might we be bedfellows? I find it difficult to sleep alone," Dudley whimpered.

"With that face, you better get used to it!" I joked. God, the harpooners would've loved that. I was excited to tell them about it tomorrow. *With that face you better get used to it, amigo!*

"Seaman Fortnight," one of the others asked while wiping snot off his face with a dirty sock, "why do you spit upon us with your words? We are hard working men, just as you are."

"You spent all day playing with a dead fish," I reminded him.

"We enjoy our leisure time, yes. If only you'd get to know us, then you would grow to love us like brothers," he said, then began clipping his toenails off with his teeth.

"He longs for glory, not kinship, not brotherhood," interrupted Dudley. "Is that not right, Fortnight? That is why you have been so desperate to earn the approval of the harpooners. You think them superior to us, for you see some strange dignity and power in their brutishness. But Fortnight, my brother, the harpooners do not cherish brotherhood either, for they too only desire glory, often to their own detriment, and to the detriment of each other. They would leave you to drown alone in the tempest without a second thought to save themselves."

"No way. Those guys are my *friends*," I said.

"They are incapable of true friendship," Dudley insisted. "But not us, Fortnight. We stick together—that's the o.s. promise. One final thing before we shut the lights, Fortnight..."

"What?" I asked.

"Remember what I told you earlier: it is all right to cry."

Dudley blew out the oil lamp and then all was dark. The men shuffled in their beds a bit before finally settling in, then all was quiet.

"Would anyone mind terribly if I masturbated?" one of them murmured in the dark.

"Oh my god, fuck this," I said, storming out of the cabin.

XXXVII.

Stubborn Captains Sink Ships

I went above the decks to sleep outside for the night when I heard a voice calling from out in the distance. It was the crew of The Unsinkable Sixty, cruising past The Vespertina once again in their much larger, much faster ship. They had yet another freshly hunted whale in tow. "Blue Crew sucks!" they yelled, then chucked a big swordfish at me. "Real mature!" I yelled back at them, plucking the swordfish out of my body.

"Ignore them!" a voice behind me said. It was one of the engineers. "What are you doing out here anyhow? You're meant to be in the ordinary seamen cabin."

"What are *you* doing out here?" I asked him, now engaged in a heated game of mental chess.

"I often find myself too troubled to sleep,"

he said. "My name is Rexington, by the way. Chief engineer. I designed this ship, you know."

"I really shouldn't be talking to you—I'm cool now," I informed the nerd.

"I'm sorry to've disturbed you, mate. I'm just bloody restless," he said. He lit up a pipe, trying way too hard to convince me he was cool. "I hope the smoke doesn't bother you, mate. I just smoke when I'm stressed, is all."

"Stressed about what?"

"Oh, don't you concern yourself with it, mate. I only worry about the integrity of The Vespertina."

"Why?" I asked.

"I'm sure you've heard rumors about your captain, aye? About his bloody stubborness? He's gone mental over that Contemptible Blue."

"Him and me both."

Engineer Rexington went on to explain that the reclusive Captain Wilhelm had had several encounters with Contemptible Blue over the years. On his most recent voyage, his whole crew had died pursuing the legendary whale, cheered on by their captain, and Wilhelm returned to shore with no Contemptible Blue and no crew.

"And here we are now, chasing the old man's prized whale, despite his last bloody encounter," Rexington said. "You know, I built this ship for endurance, and she's a sound craft when she's at her best, but she suffered quite a bit of damage on that last voyage. After Contemptible Blue roughed her up, Captain Wilhelm hit the bottle like a madman and took The Vespertina straight into an iceberg on his journey home. One of his drunker evenings, I suppose. I *told* that crazy old coot the ship was too beat up to sail again. There's the shoddy rudder, to say the least, and not to mention a number of leaks in the hold, plugged hastily shut with wedges. He's a bloody stubborn bastard, forever undaunted by the threat of

Contemptible Blue, and you know what they say: stubborn captains sink ships. It almost leaves one to ponder: at what point must a captain's orders be disobeyed, aye?"

"Are you hinting at some sort of... mutiny?" I asked.

"Never mind!" Engineer Rexington insisted. "The captain would have our heads on spears if he heard such a word! Never mind the whole lot of it!"

Engineer Rexington tried to run off but he slipped on his shoelaces and fell on his face and broke his glasses. "Aw, my glasses!" he whined. He went to stand up but when he did all of his fancy pens fell out of his front shirt pocket. "Aw, my nice pens!" he moaned. He bent over to pick them up and split his pants open. "Aw, my stupid pants!" he cried. Then he started having an asthma attack and had to rock himself back and forth on the floor saying, "Oh jeez, oh jeez," in between puffs off his inhaler. He was such a dork, oh my god. He was lucky the other harpooners weren't there.

XXXVIII.

Chilled To The Bone

Months passed and winter came swiftly and brutally, coating the deck of The Vespertina in heavy mounds of snow. The captain stayed in hiding the whole time, and rumors continued to swirl that he couldn't be trusted. Just in case they were true, I tried not to work too hard, in protest.

I found out that it was easy to make it *look* like I was working. I'd wake up every morning shortly after sunrise and go pretend to check the sails—I'd give them a quick tug and then yell out, "Sails look good, boys!" Then I'd walk around the ship holding a big crate for a while and every time I passed a crew member I'd say, "The ol' nine to five!" Then I'd go help the swabbies shovel snow by giving them advice like, "Don't fuck up shoveling." Then it was time to walk around holding a paint can for a few hours. "Kill me now!" I'd joke as I walked. After that I'd go and tie a bunch of spare rope into a big knot and spend a few hours untangling it. "I'm getting too old for this!" I'd say.

Despite never leaving his stateroom, Captain Wilhelm often gave baffling orders to the crew through his three shipmates. Every couple of weeks, he'd fire someone from the crew at random. They'd be given a life preserver and a harpoon and thrown overboard. One time, Captain Wilhelm ordered all of us to trade clothes for some reason. One day, we were only allowed to communicate through song and dance. The whole crew was left to speculate if Captain Wilhelm was losing his mind.

Although it wasn't very difficult, the

voyage was beginning to feel pointless. The whales were overfished with the great Blubber Rush and we rarely spotted any. When we did, our rivals, The Unsinkable Sixty, would swoop in and steal our kill, telling us we sucked along the way.

In those months, the engineers seemed tense and overworked. They continued to pace around the ship scribbling down notes and whispering things to each other. I'd pick up bits and pieces of their conversations here and there—things like, "Leak in the hold," and, "There's still so much I haven't seen, I don't want to die out here," and, "The fucking rudder is gonna fall off." Just a lot of technical college-boy talk. The carpenters, cooper and blacksmith seemed to always be making repairs, while groveling about "union rules."

That leak in the cargo hold that Engineer Rexington the nerd had told me about months earlier had apparently gotten worse, plus we sprang a few more leaks to boot, so chief mate Belmont always kept an ordinary seaman stationed in the cargo hold to man the pumps. "It's just gonna leak right back in!" I pointed out astutely.

The work was thankless and the weather cruel, but at least I ran in the most elite of social circles. I felt great. Growing up, everyone told me that if I wasn't dead by 25 years old I'd be in jail, even strangers. And although they were correct about that, here I was *now,* a professional whaler that everyone thought was cool.

Still, I was an ordinary seaman by rank and had to see way more of the ordinary seamen than I could stomach. Night after night I still had to sleep in their cramped, stinky quarters. Before falling asleep they'd gab about all the big plans they had for their future.

"Someday, brothers, I shall captain a ship of my very own," one of them would say.

"Yeah right!" I'd say, just being realistic.

"Someday, brothers, I shall hunt the biggest whale on all God's watery Earth," another would say.

"Not in a *million* years," I'd say, just trying to bring things back down to Earth.

"Someday," another would say, "I shall get a girlfriend."

"*Pffffffffttt*," I'd say, just trying to be the voice of reason.

Over the course of those few months, I re-told my story about killing Contemptible Blue so often that I forgot he wasn't dead, but rather still very much alive, lurking down in the briny deep and waiting to strike. Then finally, he did.

It was a cold, dark night. The bright stars danced in the sky. Okay, not "danced," but they were out. The ordinary seaman who was supposed to be on midnight lookout duty at the mast-head fell ill, probably because of how often the ordinary seamen compared open sores, plus sometimes they'd spit on each other to stay warm. The sick ordinary seaman complained of nausea and a high fever. "Could be faking it," I alerted the higher-ups, being helpful, but they shrugged me off and said they didn't want to take chances. They decided to quarantine him. Captain Wilhelm didn't believe in modern medicine. He believed sickness was God's way of weeding out the weak, so it was forbidden for the sick ordinary seaman to be treated. I suggested that, in order to maximize efficiency, they quarantine the sick ordinary seaman in the cargo hold, where he could *also* man the pumps. "Two birds, one violently ill ordinary seaman," I told them. Chief mate Belmont said it was a great idea. The sick ordinary seaman *hated* it, probably because he had poor work ethic, or maybe he was jealous *he* didn't think of it.

Somebody had to fill in on midnight lookout duty and so the mates turned to me. They burst into the ordinary seamen cabin just as I was falling asleep and chief mate Belmont yelled, "Fortnight, awaken!"

"Yes, listen to the chief mate!" insisted second mate Hobart.

"Yes, listen to the second mate—listen to the chief mate," insisted third mate Paulo.

"Why do we need three of you guys?" I asked.

"We need ye on lookout! Go now!" insisted chief mate Belmont.

I groveled for a little while, woke up the rest of the sleeping ordinary seamen to make it "fair," then finally got dressed and reported to the mast-head for lookout. It was the coldest night of my life. I have really bad Seasonal Effective Disorder, too, so it *sucked.* I tried to tell the mates that, but they said it was no excuse. Some people don't take mental illness seriously.

Towering above the decks of The

Contemptible Blue

Vespertina in the mast-head, I kept my eyes peeled on the water, looking out for any action. The sea was calm—so calm it began to lull me to sleep—but just as I was about to drift off, I noticed something out on the water. It was a tiny little sailboat, sailing peacefully along in the distance. I squinted my eyes for a closer look and realized: it was Sebastian, that mopey fisherman I'd met ten years ago. The poor guy was still alive. "Hey, Sebs!" I called out.

"Who's that!?" he called back weakly from the darkness, his voice nearly falling short of me.

"It's Captain Fortnight! From ten years ago!" I called out.

"Who?" he asked.

"Captain Stupid Idiot Who Fucked Up and Blew Up His Friend," I said.

"Oh, yes, ahoy!" he greeted me.

"Still haven't gotten eaten by Contemptible Blue yet, eh?" I asked.

"No," he yelled back sadly, his head hung low.

Just then, I noticed a strange bubbling at the surface of the water just beneath Sebastian's sailboat—thick, heavy bubbles, so big you could hear them pop. The sea seemed to be boiling. Then, suddenly, a black hole appeared just beneath Sebastian's sailboat. The boat was in an instant sucked into the black abyss, and down Sebastian went into the gaping mouth of my old foe. *My Behemoth, My Bane, My Contemptible Blue.* I heard the godawful chomping sound as old Blue chewed Sebastian and his sailboat to pieces. I was really psyched for Sebastian.

Contemptible Blue submerged back underwater, out of sight. He blew a trail of bubbles up to the surface as he circled the ship from down below. I followed the bubbles, running laps around the decks of The Vespertina. After a few laps his trail disappeared, and I waited patiently for him to show his ugly face again, clutching my harpoon gun tight and preparing to strike. Suddenly, the big blue beast rocketed out of the water, soaring straight up into the air. There he was, even bigger than I remembered. Hundreds of feet long. Ungodly, not of this Earth, seemingly invincible. *How in the world do you kill the world's largest living creature?* I wondered aloud as I watched him soar into the sky and block out the light of the moon.

Then, the *actual* largest living creature on Earth, the actual Contemptible Blue or so I hoped, came shooting out of the sea just behind the first whale, swallowed him whole and dove gracefully back into the water without a splash.

Please let that be the real Contemptible Blue this time, I thought to myself.

Heavy billows of whale blood rose to the surface. Contemptible Blue was down there, invisible beneath the cover of water but still giving me signs of his presence. Every few seconds, he'd blow some bubbles up to the surface to remind me he was there. He was taunting me. If he could speak, he'd probably say, "You'll never catch me," or, "You're a bad whaler," or, "Nice try, chowder head."

"*You're* the chowder head, actually," I yelled at the ocean.

For a brief moment I thought about alerting the rest of the crew, but decided against it. This whale was *mine* and *mine* alone for the killing. He called me a *chowder head*, for Christ's sake.

"Okay, Contemptible Blue," I whispered to myself, "I killed you once, as far as everyone knows, and I can do it again, for the first time. To the whaleboats!"

I ran starboard and lowered a whaleboat into the water below. I jumped overboard with a big splash, climbed into the whaleboat, shook the water off and began to row. "To the whaleboats!" I yelled again, even though I was already in the whaleboat.

I saw a bubbling at the surface about 20 yards out and came to a stop. I clutched my harpoon gun and waited for him to appear. "Come on, ol' Blue, you're mine," I said. "No I'm not, you confabulating fool," I imagined him saying back, which pissed me off. "*You're* the one who confabulates, actually," I yelled at the water.

Suddenly, my whaleboat was struck from beneath and I was thrust off the surface of the water and sent flying through the air. He'd given the bottom of my boat a slap with his flukes. "Real mature!" I yelled as I went flying. I fell out of the boat in mid air, still clutching my harpoon gun, and fell into the sea with a big splash. "Cannonball!" I yelled before hitting the surface, just trying to lighten things up.

I swam back up to the surface of the water, finished laughing about my funny cannonball bit, and tread water while trying to spot Contemptible Blue. My teeth clattered from the bitter cold and my limbs were so numb I could barely swim. Contemptible Blue was no where to be spotted for a few moments, then I finally saw the top of his massive, ugly head peeking out from below the depths about 100 yards out. Suddenly, he gave a quick kick of his tail and came speeding towards me like a bullet. Oh, also, I forgot to mention that the aforementioned depths were murky. They were murky depths. Anyway...

I took a deep breath, aimed my harpoon gun, and fired. "Lord, if you're up there, which you're definitely not," I whispered to the sky as my harpoon pierced the air, "please grant me the strength to kill this innocent whale that you created."

My harpoon stuck Contemptible Blue right between his eyes. He seemed completely unharmed, but submerged back underwater and out of sight again. Still clutching my harpoon gun tightly, I was pulled down into the deep along with him. The deep was briny.

I lost my bearings underwater. Immediately, I couldn't tell if Contemptible Blue was pulling me down or up or left or right. I opened my eyes for a moment and there was nothing but salty blackness. Imagine my terror. The pitch black. The bitter cold. The 600-foot whale dragging me through the depths (murky ones). The weight of the ocean above me. The icky seaweed brushing my feet down there. "Eww!" I yelled, in regards to the bad seaweed.

Suddenly, I was above the surface again, soaring through the air. Contemptible Blue had rocketed himself out of the water once again, with me still in tow. Finally, I let go of my harpoon gun, forfeiting my grasp on Contemptible Blue, and fell back down into the deep. *Welp, I'm back in the briny deep again,* I thought to myself. I was so *over* the briny deep at this point. People ask me what's the worst part about the briny deep, and I say it's definitely gotta be all the brine.

I swam back up to the surface and looked for The Vespertina. She was about 70 yards away, quickly leaving me behind. I swam furiously after her, screaming for the attention of the crew. Someone finally spotted me, struck the sails and slowed to a halt, allowing me to catch up. They tossed me down a rickety old rope ladder. I climbed aboard and collapsed onto the deck, my whole body chilled to the bone.

As the three furious shipmates crowded around me, the harpooners boarded the whaleboats and rowed off to pursue Contemptible Blue. I really hoped they wouldn't catch him, since I was supposed to have killed him ten years ago and all.

The third, second and chief mate leered down at me angrily. "Fortnight," said chief mate Belmont, his voice shaking with rage, "what were ye doing, ye fool!?"

"Yeah, answer the chief mate—what were ye doing, ye fool!?" asked second mate Hobart.

"Yeah, answer the second mate—answer the chief mate—what were ye doing, fool!?" asked third mate Paulo.

"I really feel like we only need *one* of you guys," I gurgled, still spitting up sea water.

"Answer me now, incorrigible seaman," demanded chief mate Belmont.

"Yes, answer him!" demanded second mate Hobart.

"Yes, answer them!" insisted third mate Paulo.

"I had him," I muttered.

"Ye're meant to alert the crew when a whale is spotted," cried chief mate Belmont. "Yer actions tonight were egregious, thou unruly seaman!"

"Yes, egregious!" cried second mate Hobart.

"I'm the third mate!" cried third mate Paulo.

Chief mate Belmont scowled and took a long puff off his pipe, looking contemplative. He grabbed me by the collar of my now frozen-stiff monkey jacket and lifted me up to my feet. "I think it's time ye met the captain," he said grimly.

"Great! I have some feedback for him. I think we can downsize the crew a little bit," I said, nodding subtly towards the second and third mates.

XXXIX.

The Stateroom

Chief tattletale Belmont, second tattletale Hobart and third tattletale Paulo led me below the decks and to the door of the captain's stateroom. Belmont knocked on the door and announced himself.

"A commendable job knocking on the door, chief mate Belmont," second mate Hobart said.

"Yes, *really* commendable job," third mate Paulo added.

"Third mate, how *dare* ye try and show me up like that! *Me,* the *second* mate," second mate Hobart snapped.

"Sorry, second mate Hobart!" third mate Paulo pleaded.

"...It just feels like having *one* of you guys would suffice, is all I'm saying," I said.

Then a deep, booming voice called out from behind the captain's door. "Probably the captain," I pointed out. "Ye may enter," the voice said.

Inside the stateroom, Captain Wilhelm stood with his back to me, examining a map hung on the wall. Every wall of the stateroom was plastered corner-to-corner in tattered old maps. Drained bottles of rum littered the floor. The room stunk of liquor. And cinnamon, and nutmeg. The captain was drinking a hot rum toddy. I had to try not to laugh. Just a weird drink of choice for a crazy, reclusive sea captain.

The three mates threw me to the floor and then explained to Captain Wilhelm what I had done. They also mentioned the thing I said about how we probably only needed one mate instead of three. "Tell me where I'm wrong though," I chimed in. Then the three mates walked out, slamming the door behind them and leaving me all alone with the enigmatic Captain Wilhelm.

He was an enormous, hulking man. He was hunched but still tall at 6'6", 350 lbs. Still examining his maps and showing me only his back, he asked me, "Is it true, seaman, that ye lowered for a whale without so much as alerting thy shipmates?"

I was nervous. All the rumors that I'd heard about the captain were swirling through my head, like how he was the type of captain to kill an unruly crew member without a second thought. I had to say something to get on his good side. "Have you lost weight?" I asked.

"This is the first time we've met," Captain Wilhelm pointed out.

Welp, I tried, I thought to myself. I calmed myself and quietly accepted my death. "Okay, let's do this," I said to Captain Wilhelm, trying to get my execution done and over with. "I'm thinkin' let's just do this execution style—harpoon to the back of the head." I got on my knees and put my hands behind my back. "No last words," I said to the captain.

"Seaman," he spoke, "ye must be aware by now, after months at sea aboard me beautiful Vespertina, that the bond between me crew and I is... tenuous, to say the very least. Ye've noticed by now it is seldom that I leave me stateroom."

"Yeah. Anyway, you ready to do this?

Here's my harpoon gun. Go ahead and pop one of those 'poons through my skull," I said, trying to hurry this execution along.

"In me reclusiveness I hear very little, or rather, nearly *nothing* of what is said of me behind closed doors, or rather even out in the open air of the decks," the captain said. "How me crew feels about this voyage, and how hopeful they are for a safe return, I do not know. Tell me, seaman: what've ye heard about thy captain? Is it rumored that I am a dangerous and reckless man, my judgment fogged by some strange monomania? Has it been rumored that I view me crew as disposable, competent though they may often be? Has it been asserted, up there above the hatches, that I'll stop at nothing to catch me prey?"

"Yes," I confessed. "Anyway, it's been nice meeting ya, let's go ahead and get me executed. Try to hit me right on the brain stem, if you could. Make this thing nice and quick."

Contemptible Blue

"Grand," Captain Wilhelm said. "Things are just as I hoped—me crew thinks I'm crazy. I'd always figured, seaman, that if I holed meself up in me stateroom and made sporadic, perplexing demands of me crew, then they'd presume me crazy, and out of fear of their eccentric captain, they'd break their backs for a gainful voyage. A gamesome captain commands no respect. Onto you, seaman. I have heard much about ye from me shipmates. They say ye don't work, ye just walk around holdin' a paint can."

"Umm... You're thinking of a different crew member," I lied.

The captain let out a low, guttural grunt like a hungry dog, then finally turned to face me. I recoiled at the sight of him. His face was beet red, his eyes yellow and lifeless, and he had the bulbous, ruddy nose of a decades-long alcoholic. He must have hit the hot rum toddies pretty hard over the years. "What's wrong, gallied seaman?"

he asked, noticing my disgust. He took a step towards me, then stumbled a little bit, knocked over his nightstand and fell flat on his face. "Sorry, little drunk," he confessed, hobbling back up onto his feet. Then he began fixing himself another hot rum toddy. I chuckled to myself and he asked me what was so funny but I didn't want to tell him I was laughing at his funny drink so instead I told him I was laughing at something that happened earlier and he asked me what it was so I told him about the funny "Cannonball!" bit I did earlier. "Ah. That's pretty funny," he admitted.

"Me chief mate warned me of a grim development," he continued. "One of thy fellow ordinary seamen've fallen ill and has been quarantined in the cargo hold for the crew's safety, aye?"

"Could be faking, sir," I alerted the captain.

"And still, even grimmer news has reached me ears, like rumors of a shoddy rudder or a leaky hull. Me shipmates report that the whales are overfished. And I am told our rivals, The Unsinkable Sixty, mock us and slander the name of The Blue Crew, aye?"

"They're really mean," I agreed, showing the captain my mark from when they threw that swordfish at me.

Captain Wilhelm came face to face with me, staring me directly in the eye, and grabbed me by the throat. "Tell me why, seaman, I shan't toss ye overboard right this moment for yer transgressions?"

"Well first, let me tell you my weaknesses," I said. "Number one: I blew up an entire crew once. Wait, hold on, I did that wrong."

"Blew up a whole crew? Ha ha ha! Which crew?" the captain asked, sounding delighted.

"The Confederacy for the War on Whalers."

Captain Wilhelm let go of my throat, backed away, downed his hot rum toddy and prepared another. He could barely stand up straight as he squeezed the lemon juice and ground the cinnamon. *This guy is a mess,* I thought to myself, watching him gently stir his fun cocktail.

"Ye're lyin'," he finally spoke. "I'd heard the *rumors* that ye blew up the Confederacy. Me shipmates tell me ye've been goin' around boastin' about thy triumph over Captain Meierhorn and his men. Am I really meant to believe that you, of all men, brought down The Confederacy for the War on Whalers? Ha! I do not, seaman."

"Then how do you explain *this!?*" I said as I reached into my pocket and flashed a condom at the captain—I accidentally reached into the wrong pocket. "*This,* I mean," I said, reaching into the correct pocket this time and flashing the old badge of Captain Meierhorn. Captain Wilhelm snatched it and inspected it closely.

"Well damn me soul to Hell, it's *real.* Me son's old badge."

Contemptible Blue

"Your *son's!?*"

"It's a small world, seaman Fortnight. Me eldest son always had contempt in his heart for his father, as well sheltered and well fed as I kept the boy. He grew up to found The Confederacy for the War on Whalers. The scoundrel! Took to blowin' up whaleships out of spite for his father. Gave me and me fellow whalers hell for decades."

"If it makes you feel any better," I said, "he died a truly terrible death. Just absolutely brutal."

Captain Wilhelm chuckled. "It does," he said. He downed his hot rum toddy and fixed himself yet another, stumbling all around the stateroom. "Look at me, aye Fortnight? A walkin' cliché if ever there was one. Yer typical drunken sea captain."

"Uhh, yeah," I said, instead of what I was really thinking, which was that I don't think most sea captains get wasted off hot rum toddies.

"Tell me, Fortnight," the captain continued,

"how does a sailor like thyself—one so lacking in fear, one who extirpated the Confederacy, one who is happy to lower for a whale all on his own without a single harpooner by his side—find himself in the pitiful ranks of the ordinary seamen?"

"Well, I'm *actually* more of a harpooner," I said. "You can ask the harpooner team—they think I'm cool."

"Ha ha ha!" the captain laughed. "Ye're one bloody bold bastard, indeed. 'Tis a shame ye've wasted these months doing the work of an ordinary seaman. Enough hath been said, Fortnight. May ye never be made to swab the deck or slumber among the ordinary seamen again. Ye say ye're a harpooner, so I will believe that to be so. Let's get ye a new harpoon!"

"Are you saying that I'm... I'm on the harpoon team!?" I asked.

"Aye," the captain grunted.

Contemptible Blue

I was so overcome with joy that I nearly cried. I thought back to all those harpoon store owners and police offers and therapists throughout the years who'd told me that I shouldn't be allowed to own a harpoon, and I thought to myself, *Looks like I showed you guys.*

I was excited to go tell the boys on the harpooning team that we could sleep together at night now.

XL.

The Golden Boy

The harpooners had come back empty handed after setting out to pursue Contemptible Blue earlier. He'd eluded them as he'd done so many other whalers. They were disappointed, but cheered up when they heard the good news: I made the harpoon team! Suddenly, after months of working hard, tirelessly carrying that paint can back and forth, everything was going my way. I became Captain Wilhelm's golden boy. He even began inviting me to his stateroom to dine with him for supper every night. We ate like kings, feasting on the finest quahog chowders. Meanwhile, the harpooners and engineers ate like mere common people, feeding on soggy biscuits every night. The ordinary seamen were given old fish skeletons to suck on.

"Tell me thy tale once more, Fortnight, about how ye blew the Confederacy to smithereens," Captain Wilhelm would ask me every single night.

"Fade in on a sprawling blue ocean," I'd say, putting a little theater into it. "Pan right to reveal The Confederacy for the War on Whalers' ship, bobbing up and down atop a restless ocean. Zoom in closer: I'm standing there on the main deck, dynamite in hand. Confederacy soldiers rush me to try and seize my dynamite, but I fight them off with my free hand. It doesn't even look like I'm trying that hard. I light the dynamite with my cigarette, drop it to the floor and backflip right off the deck of the ship. Right before I hit the water below I say, 'Looks like you're gonna need more *lifeboats*.' I don't even look back at the explosion when the ship blows up." The captain would clap and cheer every time I re-told the story. "Good show, lad," he'd say.

All my fellow harpooners were always asking me what the captain was like behind closed doors. In order to help Captain Wilhelm keep up the illusion that he was crazy, I'd tell the harpooners things like, "The guy's a *maniac*. He blew up his own best friend with dynamite and then re-made him out of a burlap sack and some leaves and *buried* it." Just making up the craziest shit I could think of.

Now that I was a full-time harpooner, I finally didn't have to sleep in the dingy, cramped ordinary seamen cabin anymore. At night, me and the guys on the harpooning team were always pulling pranks on the ordinary seamen losers. We'd sneak into their cabin at night and hide a dead fish under their floorboards so that it would rot and stink up the room. Unfortunately, they never noticed. It's hard to prank people who live in squalor. So, we just started beating them up instead. When we'd run into an ordinary seaman on the deck we'd slap the mop out of their hands and check them up against the mainmast. "Harpooners rule!" we'd say. We really ran that ship. We were young, sexy, brash, and in possession of deadly weapons on international waters.

We continued to have a lot of downtime, since whales were so scarce that season. We'd hang out all day and smoke behind the mizzenmast, talking about how much we hated the authoritative shipmates. "They're a bunch of freaking *narcs*," we'd say. We'd talk about which girls on the ship we wanted to get with, hypothetically, if there were any.

Then one day while we were hanging out, Engineer Rexington came over to talk to me. "Nerd spotted! Man the harpoons!" I joked, which had the other harpooners cracking up. "This guy was like, 'Nerd spotted!'" one of the harpooners repeated with a big laugh, slapping his knee at my funny joke. Oh my god we were *dying* it was so funny.

"If you're quite finished laughing at me, may I see you privately, Fortnight?" Rexington asked.

"Umm, you gotta buy me *dinner* first!" I joked, crackin' up the harpooners again. "This guy said, 'You gotta buy me dinner!'" one of them repeated. Oh my god it was all-time classic.

Finally, I followed Rexington's lead down into the blubber room. "What are we doing in here?" I asked.

"I only wanted somewhere private to speak with you, mate," Rexington said. "It's burdensome to get a minute of bloody *privacy* on this ship. But, considering how fruitless this whaling voyage has been thus far, I don't imagine anyone using the blubber room any time soon. We can speak privately here. Paulo, Hobart and Belmont won't bother us, those imbeciles. *Fools*, all three of them."

"It *does* seem like we don't need three of those guys," I concurred. "What a bunch of narcs, too."

"Now then, Fortnight," Engineer Rexington continued, "do you remember our midnight exchange months ago, outside on the foredeck? My lips were quite loose that night, if you'll remember, and I made a confidant of you, sharing some of my concerns about the future of The Vespertina. Do you remember?"

"Sort of. Something about a squeak in the gull and a salty shudder?"

"A leak in the hull and a faulty rudder."

"Yes, yes."

"Well Fortnight, let me illustrate for you a more complete picture of the matter at hand, mate, and tell you precisely what Captain Wilhelm told me before we shipped. I warned him that by my estimations, The Vespertina would only sail for seven months before she fell apart. He told me, 'If I can not assemble me a crew of men competent enough to catch me prized whale and return to shore in under seven months' time, then I am no captain at all, and a watery grave shall be well deserved.' And now, Fortnight, it's been nearly seven months, and of course we've still not raised a single whale, let alone Contemptible Blue, the captain's *prized* whale."

"Hey, things are slow with the Blubber Rush and all, but we're gonna get something soon. Harpooners rule!" I told Rexington.

"Yes, yes," Rexington said dismissively.

"Say it..." I told Rexington, punching my fist into my palm threateningly.

"Harpooners rule," Rexington admitted begrudgingly.

"Aaaand...?" I said.

He sighed. "And engineers drool," he admitted.

"Ha ha, yeah!"

"Fortnight, I do not mean to cast aspersions on this crew," Rexington continued, "but the time has come to take precautions. You seem to have become a trusted mate and confidant of the captain's. If I, or the shipmates, or anyone else on the crew were to question the captain, we'd be thrown overboard. But not you, for he has taken quite the shine to you, considering your past with The Confederacy for the War on Whalers. You might suggest to the captain that we stop ashore on a port of call—only briefly, of course—and my team and I can make the necessary repairs. We could turn west right now and reach the coast in only a week's time. It wont take a day or two to make the repairs. All of this is not to mention, Fortnight, that one of the ordinary seamen is terribly ill and still quarantined in the hold. He needs medical attention."

"I don't mean to cast aspersions, but fine, I'll try to talk to Wilhelm," I said. I already knew the expression "cast aspersions" before I heard Rexington say it. I didn't take it from him.

I went above the hatches to find a quiet, private place to think about how I should broach the subject with Captain Wilhelm, but then when I got up there, I saw that some of my harpooner buddies were making some of the ordinary seamen lick seagull[2] shit off the floor and I got distracted by that. "Ha ha ha, epic!" I said, rushing over to join in. "Harpooners rule!!!" I yelled as I grabbed Dudley and made him lick some of the shit. "I'm never gonna die!!!" I yelled up at the sky, feeling invincible.

Dudley whimpered and kind of fought back slightly, then I saw a single tear roll down his dirty cheek. "It's my birthday," I heard him say softly.

XLI.

Happy Birthday Dudley

I didn't know it was Dudley's birthday. I eased up on him a little after I found out. I've always had a soft spot for birthdays. As a child, my

---

2   That's a bird

parents often forgot mine. Literally, they often forgot I was born. I'd come home from school and they'd get startled and say, "Who the hell is that!?" and then chase me out with a newspaper. I wanted to do something nice for Dudley. The best gifts are the ones you make yourself, so I made something really, really special for Dudley: the decision to let him stop licking shit off the floor. "Happy birthday, Dudley!" I said. Then I decided, just for this *one* night, to hang out with Dudley a little bit.

After the harpooners were done making the other ordinary seamen lick seagull shit (the ordinary seamen had to fake death to ward them off), I told my teammates, "I'll catch up with you guys later!" and then hung back with the ordinary seamen. "Alright," I said to Dudley, "what do you have planned for your birthday?"

"I'll be having a lovely celebration in the ordinary seamen cabin with my fellow ordinary seamen."

"Sounds awful. I'll come along and see if I can make it fun. I know I'm hard on you and the other ordinary seamen sometimes, but I want you to understand: it's *only* because I don't care for you."

"No thank you."

"What?"

"I do not believe I'd enjoy your company. I'll be celebrating without you, lest I spend my birthday being disparaged and brutalized. Why don't you go catch up with your friends on the harpoon crew?"

One of the ordinary seamen came out holding a big dead fish with a bunch of candles in it, then everybody sang "Happy Birthday" to Dudley and he blew out the candles. He looked happy. Then, they all went back to the ordinary seamen quarters to dig into Dudley's birthday fish, leaving me behind.

Contemptible Blue

Generally I wanted nothing to do with the low-ranking ordinary seamen, but they had no right to not invite me to the party. I went outside to whack the mizzenmast with a big stick to blow off steam for a few minutes, then decided to go down to the ordinary seamen cabin and try to sneak into the party. When I got down there, they had finished eating the birthday fish and were drinking, dancing and singing sea shanties. They seemed to be having a great time, which wasn't fair. Dudley was glowing. I'd never seen someone with so many boils on his face and so many clumps of hair missing from his head look so happy. You would think there'd be an inverse relationship there.

When they heard me come into the cabin, all the ordinary seamen stopped dancing and singing and asked me to leave. "Fine, this is going to be the worst party of all time. There's not even any *girls*," I said. I slammed the door behind me and stormed out, then heard the party resume in there.

"This is the best party ever!" I heard one of them yell in there.

"Yeah right!" I yelled from outside.

I joined back up with the harpooners, who were up to their usual business of sitting around on the quarter deck, just smoking and talking about whales and women. I started to get a little bored. We had pretty much said all there was to say about the topics: we liked to hunt whales and have sex with women. We seemed to've run out of things to say. I went back and tried to sneak into the ordinary seamen party again. They were doing a conga line dance and singing and laughing. "No room for *you*!" one of them yelled at me.

"Fine! This party sucks!" I said.

"No it doesn't!" Dudley said.

Just then, Engineer Rexington appeared and pulled me aside, leading me to the blubber room. "Fortnight, have you spoken to the captain yet, mate?" he asked. "Please, Fortnight, you must not procrastinate, mate. We've not the luxury of time. You must talk some sense into him. Also, were you just partying with the ordinary seamen?"

"*Pffft*, no way! They wish!!"

"No we don't!" one of them yelled from inside the cabin.

"Well anyway," Engineer Rexington continued, "please speak with the captain by tomorrow morning. Otherwise, we'll have to take other measures."

"What sort of measures?"

"Never mind for now. Let's hope it wont come to that," Engineer Rexington concluded ominously. He walked off and I went to go and try to crash Dudley's party one last time but they chased me off with a newspaper.

XLII.

I'll Suck The Marrow Out Thy Bones

The next morning I went to Captain Wilhelm's stateroom to have that talk with him. It was tough to broach the subject without making it seem like I was questioning his authority. I decided to do a classic "compliment sandwich," which is when you say something complimentary to someone, then give them some constructive feedback, then top it off with another compliment. It's a technique I'd used before in leadership positions and on first dates and in my wedding vows.

I walked into the captain's stateroom and told him, "Hey Captain, you're looking particularly fit today. I think we should sail back to shore and get The Vespertina repaired because many peoples' lives including mine and yours are in danger. I love your coat, by the way."

"What was that, Fortnight?" the captain asked, sounding irritated.

"Great coat," I said.

"Ere that," he clarified. He was slurring his words and could hardly stand up straight. He was definitely hitting the toddies hard that morning.

"Oh, right," I said, "this is, like, *so* stupid, but I'm thinking maybe we should sail back to shore for a little while and get that leak in the cargo hold fixed. Plus, the rudder is about to fall off. Maybe we could get that fixed up. I don't know, it's *so* stupid, just forget it."

"Fret not, Fortnight. We'll ship ashore and make the repairs... just as soon as we kill Contemptible Blue and every cask in my hull is spilling over with whale oil."

"Ha ha ha, yeah, for sure," I said, trying hard to keep things light. "Definitely. Here's the thing, though, is that I'm actually just thinking: what if we fixed the ship *before* we caught a whale? I don't know, I'm just spitballin' here."

"Need I remind ye, Fortnight, that we've yet to drain a *single* whale, and I've not become a pint of whale oil richer since shipping out."

"God, I *know,* things have just been *sooo* crazy lately. We're definitely gonna get one soon though, for sure. Although, you know what? I'm just having a thought: what if we got the boat fixed real quick? That could be a fun thing for the

whole crew to do together."

My best efforts to keep things civil went out the window when, suddenly, all those warnings I'd heard about the captain became a reality. Wilhelm went from 0 to 100 in an instant, grabbing me by the neck and slamming me against the wall and screaming, "Since when do *you* give the orders around here!?"

"Captain, *please*, you're wasted—this entire ROOM smells like cinnamon!"

"If you and those lazy harpooners—those arrogant hunks—cared about anything other than thy social ranking, then ye'd have caught me that whale months ago, and we'd be back home on dry land in the warm company of our loved ones. Did thy teammates catch me that whale that you thyself pursued weeks ago? Nay! Ye haven't caught me so much as a *marlin.* It is just as I told that *rat* of an engineer, Rexington: if this godforsaken crew can't catch me a whale and fill me casks in seven months' time, then may we *all* sink. Now exit my quarters, ascend to the decks and go kill Contemptible Blue."

"But there might be a mutiny!" I blurted out.

"What?" the captain asked, speaking in a low growl as he threw me to the floor. "Did ye just say what I think ye said? Did ye just murmur of a... mutiny?"

I tried to backpedal: "No no no, I said, uhh... 'hootenanny.' There might be a *hootenanny* later. Should be fun."

"If any poor bastard wishes to strip me of me rank—to overthrow and disgrace me on me own ship—then ye go ahead and ye tell them, Fortnight, that I am right here in me stateroom, just below the hatches, unarmed, unguarded and unwilling to go down without a fight. Ye tell them they can march down here right now, or *whenever* they please, and try their hand at this mutiny, but please assure them, Fortnight, that they shan't be leavin' this stateroom alive. *I'll suck the marrow out of their brittle bones.* And the same fate shall befall you too if ye side against me. Cross me and

I will suck the marrow out thy bones, so make peace with thy god."

"Um, actually, I'm an atheist. I don't necessarily believe in the afterlife as it's described biblically and—"

"No one cares, Fortnight."

"Oh okay."

The captain's threat was a little concerning. Sure, we *all* say things we don't mean in moments of passion. We've *all* told somebody we'd suck out their bone marrow because we were angry—I had written those exact words in a message-in-a-bottle just that morning—but I think Captain Wilhelm actually meant it.

I got up off the floor, dusted myself off and went to exit the captain's stateroom. Just as I was about to leave, Captain Wilhelm stopped me. "Fortnight," he called out, "one final, nagging matter to discuss, ere ye leave."

"Yeah?"

"The sick ordinary seaman quarantined in the cargo hold..."

"What about him?"

"He's not going to make it, lad. We can not run the dire risk of his escape, for that putrid disease of his, whatever it is, may spread to the rest of me crew. He is in anguish. It would seem to me, Fortnight, that the humane thing would be to end the poor rube's misery."

"Dudley has some secret potion that—"

"Nay! You are a harpooner, are ye not?"

"Big time," I said, pantomiming shooting a harpoon.

"Then *harpoon*. Put the poor bumpkin out of his misery, and do so *tonight*. Ye're excused," Captain Wilhelm concluded. Then he took off his captain's jacket and changed into a nice dress shirt and said, "I'll be up shortly for that hootenanny."

I left the captain's stateroom feeling pretty stressed out from having been ordered to execute a man. Plus, now I had to plan an entire hootenanny.

I went to Engineer Rexington's cabin and told him what happened. "I see," he said calmly. "That is certainly not the response I was hoping for, but I can not say the captain's words shock me. Thank you for speaking to the captain. I do not believe there is any more work to be done by you. None more at all. Aside from... *you know...*"

"What?"

"Well, Fortnight, *you* have orders from the captain to harpoon the sick ordinary seaman, and you answer to him as your highest authority, do you not? Personally, I am curious to see how you take such an order. It should be quite a good test of what sort of man you are, and of what we can expect from you in the near future. Run along now, mate," Engineer Rexington concluded ominously. I was getting pretty sick of all of Rexington's ominous alluding. "Just talk regular!" I yelled to him before angrily storming out of the room.

XLIII.

An Order Is An Order

An order is an order, I thought to myself as I marched down to the cargo hold to put the sick ordinary seaman out of his misery.

The leaks in The Vespertina's hold had indeed worsened, flooding the hold with icy cold ocean water. I went in there and the water was up to my waist. The sick ordinary seaman was doing a bad job of pumping the water out of the hold like he'd been ordered to. I found him floating in the water on his back, moaning like a sick dog. I guess he was on break. He was pale and emaciated, looking back at me with vacant eyes. He was in bad shape. "I got promoted to harpooner!" I told him, trying to cheer him up. It didn't seem to work. He must have been jealous.

The sick ordinary seaman steadied himself on his feet, the frigid ocean water reaching up to his chest, and tried to speak but couldn't. He could only moan and cough and reach his hand out as if to ask for help. "Look buddy," I told him, "I know you're sick, but I have good news that I think should cheer you up: I'm here to kill you." His eyes grew as wide as saucers and welled up with tears.

With trembling hands, I clutched my harpoon gun, my finger on the trigger, and prepared to do "the humane thing." His pathetic, miserable gaze sent a chill down my spine. The cold, hollow silence down there in the hold was deafening. More deafening than the vengeful sea at her stormiest. More deafening than the roar of the mighty blue whale at her angriest. More deafening than a singles cruise at its most-being-bombed.

I felt my grip loosen on my harpoon gun. It seemed completely out of my control, like my hands had a mind of their own. My harpoon gun fell from my hands and I watched it splash in the water and sink to the floor. "Listen," I told the sick ordinary seaman with a sigh, "I've decided not to kill you, and it's *not* because I'm afraid to harpoon you. I'm just a little tired. And plus I'm sick, and my hand hurts a little. Plus I'm busy. I'm gonna come back tonight and let you out of here. You go *straight* to the lifeboats and *scram*. And if you tell anyone about this, you're gonna *wish* I harpooned you to death."

I turned around to leave, feeling pretty good about my exit. *You'll WISH I harpooned you to death, amigo!* Then I heard the ordinary seaman behind me let out some awful, strange gurgling noise from his throat. I looked back at the twitchy seaman. He was foaming at the mouth and his eyes had gone completely white. He lunged towards me, growling like an animal, and grabbed my arm and sunk his teeth into my flesh. We both toppled over, plunging down into the waist-high water. As I tried to kick him off me, I felt around the floor for my harpoon gun. He got a few more bites in before I finally found it. I clobbered him over the head with the harpoon gun and knocked him out cold, then I quickly fled the hold and locked the door behind me. I stuck a sign on the door that said, "Do not enter: seaman flood," so that no one would go in there. I laughed at my funny sign for a few hours and then left.

XLIV.

Sex With A Woman

Almost immediately after my encounter with that sick ordinary seaman, I started to feel ill, but there was an even bigger concern at hand: a sudden, strange change in the social atmosphere aboard The Vespertina. I went to go meet up with my harpooner friends up on the quarter deck and they gave me the cold shoulder, acting like they didn't even see me. When I tried to talk to them, they pretended not to hear me. "Sex!" I screamed, thinking that would get their attention, but it didn't. "With a *woman*," I clarified. Still nothing. I was baffled. Probably the ordinary seamen were spreading rumors about me because they were jealous of my popularity. I stormed down to their cabin, where I found them massaging each other's dirty, bare feet, to interrogate them. "Hey you seamen freaks," I said, "what's up with the harpooners? They don't think I'm cool anymore. What did you say to them?"

They too pretended not to hear me. It didn't make any sense. I slammed the door and stormed off. I went back up to the main deck where I bumped into one of the engineers. "What's up, dork-gineer?" I said, just trying to exchange pleasantries, and even *he* ignored me.

I was pissed off and I needed to blow off some steam so I went to go beat up the steward, but then on the way I ran into Dudley. He seemed stressed out, probably because he was in his 40's and still a virgin (presumably). He looked around to make sure no one was watching and then grabbed my hand and led me to the blubber room to speak privately.

"Fortnight," Dudley whispered to me, "I am not meant to be speaking to you, and I do so against my better judgment, so please heed my words, for this favor that I am so cautiously granting you may save your life. Fortnight, several months ago, before the weather turned dismal and The Vespertina donned her white coat of winter, I told you that ordinary seamen are always there for one another, for that is the o.s. promise. Well, you may have ascended the ranks to harpooner, and you have certainly adopted their taste for bullydom, but I knew you as an o.s. when first we met, and still now, all these months later, I see you as such, for I still sense a softness in your heart, despite all your efforts to smother it. I understand peer pressure has made a brute of you. Listen closely: if you wish to live to see your next voyage, and your next and your next, then board one of The Vespertina's lifeboats, abandon ship and row yourself ashore. Depart this ship and find another. May better fortune befall you on your next voyage, and may that next voyage be one unto which Herman Melville himself could not do justice with mere words."

Contemptible Blue

"Who's Herman Melville?" I asked.

"Listen to me, Captain. It has been proposed by Engineer Rexington that a mutiny had ought to occur, and to occur sooner rather than later. We spoke of it privately this afternoon—the whole crew—and nary a single man among us had any objections, for we all suspect that our well-being is of no concern to Captain Wilhelm. As you have become friendly with the captain, the crew has agreed to sever all bonds with you, for you have closely aligned yourself with an enemy—a man who poses a grim threat to his own vessel and to every man who works on her decks. It has been agreed upon by the crew, Fortnight, that if you attempt to thwart this mutiny, then you too shall be harpooned just the same as the captain. Hear this dire warning, ponder it, and do what thou wilt. I must go. And when you get back ashore, Captain, you had ought to visit a doctor, for you look ill."

I was getting sick of all the "dire warnings" around here. I'm fine with a warning here and there, but a *dire* warning!? No thanks!!! Anyway, back to my impending death...

I wasn't exactly sure what to do next. I didn't have a single friend on the entire ship. Even the seagulls seemed to be looking at me funny. *Don't be silly, the seagulls love you,* I tried to reassure myself, then one of them swooped down and pecked me in the eye. Things were grim.

The crew of The Vespertina outnumbered Captain Wilhelm and myself 20 to 2, and I was feeling sicker with every passing second. I recognized the symptoms. I'd felt the same ones long ago on The S.S. Captain Fortnight's Big Boat, and I knew what was to inevitably follow.

Ocean madness had yet to kick in, so I still had the good sense to side with the crew against Captain Wilhelm. I took a deep breath and quietly prepared myself for the two possible outcomes of what was soon to follow: successfully mutinying Captain Wilhelm, or witnessing yet another massacre at sea that kills a bunch of my friends. *Whaling fucking blows,* I thought to myself.

XLV.

Hootenanny

It was nearly midnight. The crew was fast asleep. Even the seaman on duty at the mast-head had been lulled into slumber. I'd have to be sure to get him fired just as soon as the mutiny was over. I was nauseous and my skin burned hot, even out there in the sub-zero open air, but I scrounged up the energy to climb up the main-sail until I towered above the deck of The Vespertina where everybody could hear my cries. "Whale!" I yelled, trying to get their attention.

Seconds later, the whole crew was out on the main deck—chief mate Belmont, second mate

Hobart, third mate Paulo, the harpooners, the ordinary seamen, Jojo the cook, Cooper the blacksmith, Black Smith the cooper, the carpenters, Herschel and even the engineers, although Engineer Rexington was strangely absent. He was probably busy doing engineer stuff, like inspecting an abacus underneath a microscope, which is my best understanding of what his job was.

Chief mate Belmont noticed me up on the main-sail and yelled up to me, "Whale ho?"

"Well, no," I said. "I have a dramatic proclamation to make!"

"Ye look ill, Fortnight," chief mate Belmont said.

"Listen to me, noble Blue Crew! With the exception of a few of you—the mates, the ordinary seamen, Jojo, that nondescript little boy character, Black Smith, Cooper, the carpenters, the engineers —I've come to think of you all as my dear friends!

Contemptible Blue

I've heard murmurings of a mutiny! I'm not gonna say who snitched on you guys and told me about the mutiny—let's just leave Dudley out of this! I understand you think I'm on the captain's side! Sure, he and I have shared meals together. Yes, I've become his main confidant and we've often conversed late into the night. Yes, we both agreed that if we're both still single when we're 45 then— never mind. The point is this: my relationship with the captain has soured! He's a reckless drunk who can't put the toddy down! I stand with *you,* Blue Crew! I say let's toss that lush to the sharks! Let's take control of this ship, before he sails us all straight to our grave! What do you say?"

I waited for applause, but none came. Then, chief mate Belmont cried out, "Ye've been an unruly and most perfidious seaman since day one of this voyage, Fortnight, ye incorrigible buffoon! And now ye show symptoms of ocean madness! Look at ye! Thy mouth foams like briny, yellow billows of salt water upon the sandy shore! 'Tis not worth the risk!"

"Yeah, 'tis not worth the risk!" cried second mate Hobart.

"Yeah, 'tis not worth the risk!" cried third mate Paulo.

"What do you guys even *do*!?" I asked the mates.

"Take him out!" yelled all three mates in unison. My old friend Darius raised his harpoon gun, aimed and shot. I only narrowly avoided the harpoon, but lost my footing on the rigging of the main-sail and fell. "Cannonball!" I yelled as I fell, just trying to lighten up the mood before dying. I crashed to the deck and heard all my bones crack. The crew circled around me, staring down at me with cold eyes. I calmed myself and quietly accepted my death. "Welp, go ahead and do it," I whimpered. "No last words. No will, either. Just throw all my shit off the boat or whatever."

Contemptible Blue

As I waited for them to put me out of my misery, images of Contemptible Blue flooded my brain. The thought of him made my blood boil. I imagined what he would say to me in that moment if he could. "Looks like I won, chowder head," he might say. "My head is *normal!*" I asserted aloud, which kind of confused the crew. I felt a wave of adrenaline course through my veins, thinking about my unfinished business with the whale. Then I grimaced and thought to myself, *No, I do NOT accept my death.*

Just then, I heard Captain Wilhelm's voice bellow out from afar. "Evenin', lads," he said calmly. The whole crew gasped when they saw that he'd finally emerged from his stateroom. His mouth and shirt were stained red with blood. "I heard there was some sort of hootenanny," he said.

Captain Wilhelm was wielding a harpoon gun in each hand and chewing casually on what looked like a human bone. He spit it out onto the floor of the deck and said, "That warbly, wormish Rexington's bones were not nearly so dense as I'd dreamed. I've been drinkin' hot rum toddies since ere the sun rose and I feel *crazy*. Are they true, these rumors that've reached me ears, that there's some sort of *mutiny* at hand? If so, ye'd better make it quick, lads. I just returned from the helm. I've decided to steer us on a more thrilling route," he concluded, then pointed forward, and there ahead of us we saw a gigantic iceberg, towering above the surface of the water and casting an ominous shadow over the decks of The Vespertina. We were making a path straight towards it. That's when I finally, fully understood Captain Wilhelm: he was an insane man who didn't know he was insane but had been *pretending* to be insane to make people *think* he was insane, which he was. Interesting guy. Anyway, back to the impending mass murder...

"Now then," Captain Wilhelm continued,

"which one of ye mutinous crewmen of mine would like to offer thy delicious bones to thy noble, hungry captain? How about you, chief mate Belmont?"

Captain Wilhelm fired a harpoon square threw Belmont's ribs, sending him crumbling to the floor. We watched the color quickly drain from his face as he writhed around under the pale glow of the moon. "My muse!" cried second mate Hobart, before he too took one of Captain Wilhelm's harpoons through the ribs. "*My* muse!" cried third mate Paulo, before meeting the same fate.

Then all hell broke loose when the harpooners drew their harpoon guns and began firing harpoons wildly at Captain Wilhelm. Wilhelm, with the impossible agility of a much soberer man, dodged every harpoon as he ran starboard and hopped into the foremost whaleboat suspended on the side of the ship, ducking down for cover. The harpooners fired more harpoons, which pierced straight through the whaleboat, leaving it dotted with holes like a block of swiss cheese. *Great, now I'm hungry*, I thought to myself. The harpooners rushed starboard toward the whaleboat to confirm that they had hit Captain Wilhelm, but found that he'd miraculously disappeared. They looked around dumbfoundedly for a moment, then a bunch of them took harpoons to the back, courtesy of Captain Wilhelm, who had sneakily jumped overboard, swam underneath The Vespertina and climbed back aboard on the port side. The remaining, unharmed harpooners fired more harpoons back at Wilhelm and he ducked behind a capstan for cover. Harpoons ricocheted off the capstan as the captain cackled to himself from behind it. He leaned out from behind his shelter for a moment and fired off two more shots, taking out two more harpooners, then made a path towards the mast-head and climbed up it, dodging harpoons even as he climbed. From the great height of his mast-head, which now functioned as more of a sniper tower, he fired off more shots and took out the remaining harpooners.

At this point, the whole rest of the crew pretty much flew into a panic as Captain Wilhelm wildly fired more harpoons down at them from on high. A massive brawl broke out over who would be taking the lifeboats, because there weren't enough of them to accommodate the whole crew. A very pitiful nerd fight broke out between the engineers. They snapped each other's suspenders and threw clipboards and pens at each other and tried to un-part each other's hair as if that was some sort of crushing blow. Jojo the cook came out and just started throwing knives around. He loved it. He took out a bunch of the carpenters. Cooper the blacksmith and Black Smith the cooper wrestled one another on the floor. They had always kind of resented each other over the confusing name thing. Herschel the little boy steward was just running around whackin' people in the knees with a marlinspike.

While the crew slugged it out over who would be saved, the ordinary seamen calmly lowered the lifeboats, boarded them and sailed peacefully away atop the gentle, moon-bathed open ocean.

I was ducked behind the windlass for cover from Wilhelm's torrent of harpoons as I watched the ordinary seamen sail off. Then, Dudley looked back at The Vespertina, and I waved goodbye. He stuffed his dirty hand into his pocket, took something out and threw it to me. I caught it—it was his glass jar of strange, purple medicine. I downed the bottle. He tried to throw me his copy of the Bible too but I caught it and threw it back to him. 30 seconds later, they had disappeared safely into the night, untouched by the mayhem that had broken out aboard The Vespertina.

Contemptible Blue

I peaked out from behind the windlass to survey the damage. The entire crew, save for a few wounded carpenters and Herschel the little boy, had been taken out, either by Wilhelm's harpoons or by each other. The deck of The Vespertina ran red with blood. Captain Wilhelm had finally run out of ammo, and was calmly descending the mast-head back down to the deck.

Amid all the mayhem, I had almost forgotten about the impending iceberg crash. We were 30 seconds away from crashing into it, which would guarantee total destruction of The Vespertina. As I was deliberating whether or not to jump overboard, I noticed another craft sailing just behind us. They made way and caught up with us, sailing abreast The Vespertina now. It was The Unsinkable Sixty, our old rivals, in their dashing Poseidon. They had three freshly slaughtered whales in tow. "Ha ha ha," I heard one of them laugh from the deck of The Poseidon. "The Blue

Crew's gone mad! They're gonna crash into the iceberg! Blue Crew sucks!"

"*Ignore them*," I heard Captain Wilhelm say calmly. He was back on the main deck now, basking in the violent mess he'd made of The Blue Crew.

Then, something more spectacular caught my attention—a massive, bluish hump sticking out above the surface of the water, trailing just behind The Unsinkable Sixty. It was, unmistakably, the hump of my oldest foe. *My Behemoth, My Bane, My Contemptible Blue.*

With one quick and effortless kick of his tail, Contemptible Blue darted forward, his mouth agape, and bit The Poseidon in half. He turned over on his back contentedly as he chewed the aft half of The Poseidon to pieces, while the forward half of the ship became flooded and quickly sank as the screams of the not-so-unsinkable Unsinkable Sixty disappeared into the muffling depths of the frosty black ocean. *That's what you get for throwing a swordfish at me. Unsinkable Sixty sucks!!!* I thought to myself.

With about 15 seconds to go before we collided with the iceberg, Captain Wilhelm stood tall on the bow, the cold winter wind blowing through his hair, and watched calmly as the iceberg drew nearer and nearer. A gentle snow began to fall, turning the proud captain's head frosty white. Meanwhile, Contemptible Blue swallowed up the final remnants of The Poseidon, then turned his sights towards The Vespertina. Opening his mouth wide again, he gave another kick of his tail and came torpedoing straight towards us from the rear, ready to scoop us up straight into his throat and swallow us down.

With certain death both lying in front of and tailing behind me, I had two options to consider: remain planted on The Vespertina and die by iceberg, or submit to the foe I wasted over ten years pursuing.

Ultimately, I decided that he had earned the victory. Seconds before collision with the towering mountain of ice that lay before us, I leaped astern and went plunging into the black hole of Contemptible Blue's gaping, monstrous maw, and blacked out as the overwhelming organic darkness overtook me.

XLVI.

Onion Island

I became conscious again, and when I opened my eyes everything was pitch black. I couldn't see a thing there in my strange, squishy, meaty prison. It felt like being back in the womb, which triggered a primal fear of being trapped. I panicked and started kicking and squirming but the warm, wet walls of my gooey jail cell overwhelmed me. I could hardly move my body, and yet I felt some vague sense of movement.

I felt myself being squeezed forward, like being pushed through a narrow, slimy tube. Then, although my eyes were closed and too sticky to open, I could sense light beyond my eyelids, and suddenly I felt a new warmth—the nurturing warmth of the morning sun. I heard the peaceful chirping of birds and the gentle sloshing of waves all around me. I wiped the goo out of my eyes and opened them. There I lay in the warm sand, with a vast jungle scape before me and a vaster ocean behind me. I was beached. Some sort of gooey film and strange chunks of what looked like flesh wet the sand around me. I looked back into the ocean behind me and saw Contemptible Blue swimming off into the distance. He finally submerged back into the deep and disappeared. He'd regurgitated me onto this beach and left me to fend for myself. *Joke's on you*, *idiot*, I thought to myself, *I LOVE the beach. Waves, rays and babes, baby!* I was in for a big surprise, though.

I stood up on wobbly legs, feeling exhausted but otherwise okay. Dudley's strange purple potion had worked its magic and my sickness was gone. I wished I could thank him, but he owed me a favor anyway for giving him that nice birthday gift (not having to lick shit).

There was about 75 yards of beach between the shore and the jungle. I walked along the coast for hours and hours until I reached that same mess of whale vomit in the sand again. That's when I realized it was an island, and I'd just walked a full lap around it. I collapsed into the sand, beginning to panic.

A familiar smell hung in the air. It was the smell of onions. I walked inland a little bit to trace the source of the smell. I discovered that wild onion plants infested the entire jungle. The smell stung my eyes and nose and I struggled to keep myself from tearing up. Finally, I couldn't hold it anymore. The floodgates opened and the tears poured down my face.

Through my tears I noticed that some of the wild onion bulbs seemed to have been trampled. I noticed footprints in the dirt. There were other people here. I tried to stop crying again, in case it was girls.

"It's all right to cry," I heard a voice call out from the distance. I felt a panic and ran back towards the beach, but didn't dare go in the water with Contemptible Blue still lurking out there. I guess that was when I truly, finally realized he'd won.

The strange voice called out again, "Let me get a look at ye." It sounded barely human. I froze up as I heard a rustling in the jungle, drawing nearer and nearer. Finally, a man emerged from the thick of the jungle, squashing an onion bulb beneath his foot. He wore a dirty, tattered monkey jacket. His hair and beard, thickly clumped with mud, reached his torso. His skin was ghostly white, his eyes too. He foamed at the mouth, looking like the poster boy for ocean madness.

"Where am I?" I asked the rabid looking man.

"Onion Island."

"What is this?"

"This is where he spits us out."

"Am I in Hell?"

"No. Ye can kill yerself whenever ye'd like."

"Who are you?"

"Blagg."

Blagg. Years and years ago, dozens and dozens of deaths ago, I'd heard that name. I thought hard, then finally it came to me: it was the name of Kragg's stepbrother. The man Kragg had set out to find ten years ago. "I know someone who was looking for you," I told the man.

"Well, they'll never find me. Nor will they *you*," Blagg huffed.

"What?" I asked.

"I'm hungry," Blagg said desperately. Then, he began to charge me, growling about how he was going to eat me. I managed to elude him and escape into the jungle. I tore through the thick of onion bulbs, barely able to see through my tears. About a quarter mile in, I felt a sudden, piercing pain around my ankle and was flung into the air. I'd been caught in some sort of net trap. I swung to and fro by the ankle, until I fished the decades-old badge of Captain Meierhorn out of my monkey jacket pocket. It was dull, but with a few minutes of work I was able to saw through the net. I fell to the ground, knocking the wind out of myself. I managed to stand, nauseous and dizzy, and regain my composure, then I heard a rustling behind me. Captain Blagg showed himself again and pursued me further into the jungle. I managed to ditch him, before falling into a carefully concealed hole trap he'd dug into the ground. It was too deep to climb out of, so I had to dig a tunnel that ran parallel to the ground above and then slowly curved up to the surface. Upon finally escaping the hole trap, I heard a rustling again, followed by the hungry growl of Captain Blagg, and pushed further and further into the dense jungle scape of Onion Island.

It's been a few years since Contemptible Blue spat me out here on Onion Island. All throughout my whaling years, people alluded to Contemptible Blue being "not of this Earth," swearing that he was smarter than any other living creature—that he was some sort of incorruptible, omnipotent force, merely inhabiting the *shell* of a whale. After all these years on Onion Island—after thousands and thousands of hours of deep, thoughtful reflection—I've gone back and forth on whether or not I believe that to be the truth. At times, I do believe Contemptible Blue knew exactly what he was doing when he spat me out on Onion Island, where the hunter has become the hunted. At times I think he *revels* in the irony of stranding me on Onion Island—a place where I can't help but to cry all the time—after all my years of trying to avoid the sad sense of emptiness that probably led me to the whaling life in the first place.

But at other times, I think Contemptible Blue is more like me. That he never really had a plan. That he's just drifting chaotically and begrudgingly through a contemptible blue world that he never asked to be born into, trying to make the best of it all and occasionally sinking a few ships along the way.

I won't say Onion Island is a *great* place to live. I have to feed entirely on onions, and I'm constantly on the run from Captain Blagg, fellow casualty of Contemptible Blue. He's got the whole island booby trapped and I'm constantly chewing through net traps or digging myself out of holes, but in a way, I feel like I've been doing that my entire life.

I can enjoy the quieter moments, at least. With all my downtime I've finally been able to finish *Moby Dick.* It turns out they all die at the end. I probably should have read the whole thing before deciding to become a whaler. I have a lovely little onion garden on the south shore that I tend to. I made myself a wife out of sticks and onions, although we don't really get along.

If I'm looking on the bright side, I guess Onion Island has just the right amount of excitement. Just as you're getting bored of reflecting on your mistakes or making love to your onion wife—BOOM!—there's Blagg, trying to smash your head in with a huge rock.

Contemptible Blue

Two weeks ago, as I sprawled out in the hot sand of Onion Island, keeping an ear out for the rustlings of Captain Blagg, I saw old Contemptible Blue in the offing, swimming sluggishly towards Onion Island. He looked more porcupine than whale—he had hundreds and hundreds of harpoons sticking out of his back. Some brave whaler had gotten him real good. The winded leviathan finally reached the shore of Onion Island and beached himself in the sand. There he lay before me, blood trickling down his massive body as he moaned desparingly, staring me dead in the eye. He looked defeated, and in that moment, I knew he wasn't so immortal after all.

I plucked one of the harpoons out of his body. I noticed a price tag dangling off the end of it. I ripped it off and inspected it. It was from Fishy Al's, the harpoon store I used to work at. For all I knew, I was the man who sold the harpoons that were now slowly killing Contemptible Blue right before my very eyes. I plucked the rest of the harpoons out of his body, and then I noticed the faintest hint of a smile on his face. I gave him a nod and then, harpoon-free, he slowly inched his way back into the water and swam off. I watched his enormous hump shrink smaller and smaller as he swam further and further away, and then, just as he was almost out of sight, I watched him get bit in half and swallowed by a whale that dwarfed him in size. Maybe *that* was the *real* Contemptible Blue of legend, but I've seen enough by now to know that there's always something bigger out there.

Just then I felt a spear whiz past my ear. *The ol' nine to five!* I thought to myself as I ran for my life down the coast, Captain Blagg trailing just behind me.

That stupid idiot will never catch me. Maybe the truth is that I *can't* be caught. That I can't be killed, at least not by mortal man. That I'm smarter than any other creature on Earth, and am therefore *always* one step ahead. That bloodthirsty sailors have tried to kill me for decades but have been eluded or destroyed at every turn. If these things weren't true, would I have survived what I survived? Old Captain Fortnight lives to see another day. To dodge harpoon after harpoon and leave a trail of disarray (mere collateral damage) in his wake, for some creatures were simply built to survive against all odds. Yes, old Contemptible Captain Fortnight lives on, while others sink to the bottom of the sea, fall ill or otherwise get weeded out.

Contemptible Blue

Important Epilogue

I've written this entire story out in rocks on the beach of Onion Island. It's taken me years to find enough rocks, and to carefully arrange them into the words you're reading now. The cover was especially difficult. I wrote my story out in the hopes that one day somebody will discover Onion Island, find my story and put it into novel form. If you are that person—the selfless soul who's taken on the task of publishing my story—please read this epilogue carefully. After years of writing this story I've decided that, in retrospect, I made some poor story choices. I'd really like to make some edits. It's very hard for me to edit a story written in rocks, so please make the following changes to my story on my behalf before publishing the novel.

Please make it so that I kill Contemptible Blue in the end. Also, please name the novel *Captain Fortnight's Brave Whaling Adventure*

Contemptible Blue

Against Contemptible Blue and Captain Fortnight Wins. Do not take liberties with this!

Get rid of the part where I accidentally kill Kragg.

Please write some female characters into the novel. Whaling is a male dominated field so I simply didn't meet any along my journey, but please throw some in there. Maybe make Captain Wilhelm a girl? Also, make it so that I have a girlfriend. I should probably have sex once.

I meant to tackle race in this thing, but I forgot. Please fix!

Please add a 25,000-26,000 word-or-so chapter about the history of harpoon manufacturing in the United States. It's pretty interesting stuff. Maybe start the novel with it.

Please explicitly state what year it is, or at least what century.

Please make it clear what I look like.

Please cut out the first 39 chapters of the

novel. I wasn't really a good whaler when that stuff happened. The story should start right after I've become a well respected harpooner on The Blue Crew that everyone thinks is cool. It will be a short book.

Please cut out all the parts where I'm mean to the ordinary seamen. Make it so that I'm nice to them.

To summarize, the novel should go as follows: there's a 26,000-word opening chapter about the history of harpoon manufacturing in the United States, then we ease into a story about me, a guy with a girlfriend who gets a job on a whaleship and is good at it right away. Plus the book tackles race.

Alright, as I read back over this epilogue, I'm realizing the novel needs more work than I originally thought. I think it'd be best for me to scrap the whole thing and start fresh. I'll take another pass at it. Let's hold off on publishing the novel for now, until I get it right. I repeat: DO NOT PUBLISH THIS NOVEL IN ITS CURRENT FORM! IT'S BAD!!

Made in United States
North Haven, CT
20 December 2021

13386721R00212